A Mafia's Angel

S.E Robin

ISBN: 978-1-0684701-4-1

The Damaged Sinners of New York - Book 2 A Mafia's Angel

By S.E Robin

Edited By: From Beginning to The End
Cover Designer: GetCovers
Formatter: Chris Reilly

"Give a girl the right shoes,
and she can conquer the world."

- Marilyn Monroe

Content Warning

Reader discretion advised. +18 years

The Damaged Sinners of New York series and all books contained within this series are all works of fiction. Due to the nature of this series, some content in these books may be disturbing or triggering for some readers.

This book is not to be used as a resource for sexual education or as an informational guide to any sexual acts. Activities within this book are dangerous and are not meant to represent realistic expectations of sexual activity.

You are about to enter the dark world of the Romano Mafia, as such this book contains scenes that some readers may find triggering. The triggers contained within this book are listed below but not limited to;

Torture and murder
Blood
Water-boarding
Explicit sexual scenes
Anal play
Spitting- consensual

Kidnapping- off page in past
Contract marriage/ forced marriage

If you are happy with that or a reader like myself who likes to go in without looking, then sit back, relax, and enjoy.

Important notes:
Translations:

Fratello> pronounced: fraf-TEL-loh> brother
La Madrina> pronounced: lah mah-dree-nah> The God Mother

Chapter 1

Rosie

I WAKE AFTER TOSSING and turning all night, the nightmares from my past haunting me yet again. They stopped years ago, but after all that has happened recently, it seems to have brought them back. Turning my head, I look over and see I am not alone. I smile when I see Gabe is still asleep on the bed beside me. The room has been transformed into a makeshift hospital room, complete with machines, but the décor says otherwise.

Oil paintings of sunflowers line the burned orange walls, making the room feel dark, but the big chandelier above provides light, glass droplets sparkle when the lights are on and bounce off the offensive wall. What's odd is that at night when the chandelier is on, this room is not as dingy. The sparkling light reflecting off the walls brings the oil paintings to life, and the breeze that filters through from the French doors is surprisingly comforting.

Gabe shifts in the bed, stretching and distracting me from my thoughts as the white sheet slips down his broad chest. My eyes wander as I think about what it would be like if it were my hands stroking his chest like the sheets that move lower...

So, I am jealous of bedsheets now.

"Hey, how are you?" he asks, his voice still sleepy and sexy as sin. Dipping my head, my cheeks blush as he looks me up and down. I don't know why I am still shy around him. We have been in this room together for almost six months, and we've spoken every day, but there is something about him that turns my insides into mush. All the ways I could communicate seem to vanish, and I look like a complete idiot.

"Yeah, good, you?" I mumble as I get out of bed and hurry from the room to avoid hearing his answer.

"Woah, watch where you're fucking going." Frankie laughs as she holds on to my arms. "Are you making your escape again?" She rolls her eyes dramatically.

Sighing heavily, I look at the beauty in front of me, closing my eyes and just wishing I had the confidence she does. "Look, it's easy for you to say, but have you ever been in a room with someone like him?" I point toward the door.

"Oh, honey, I have been in a room with someone so much fucking better." She winks and leads me toward the kitchen, grabbing herself a mug and gesturing for me to sit. "Look, you have been in there for months, and I think it's time for you to say something. It's obvious you like him, and he likes you too." Her brow raises.

"I don't think so. You know as well as I do it's Sophia he is interested in, the way they look at each other... He will never see me that way." I look at her and shrug, resigned to the fact that the man I have fallen in love with will always be out of reach from me. "There is so much about me he doesn't know, and I don't even know where to start with all that sh- rubbish," I start to swear but stop myself, the nightmare still weighing heavy on my shoulders.

"You also need to sort that shit out too. You'll feel so much better getting it off your chest. If you want to say fuck, say fuck, if someone is being a dick, tell them." She smiles as if it's the easiest thing in the world.

"Yeah, well, that's easy for you to say." Taking the coffee she poured, I pull it toward me and take a sip, the bitterness instantly relaxes me.

"Okay, first she's his therapist...and I would like to add, yours too! He is not interested in her. God knows why Nico hired her. Apparently, she's the best in the *business*, but she is what you would call a twunt." She looks at me and winks. "All that aside, it looks like we have things we need to work on. Let's go." She snatches the mug away from me and grabs my hand, leading me toward the door when we are stopped in our tracks.

"I didn't think she was coming here anymore?" I look at Frankie and see the hatred in her eyes as she looks at the woman.

"Oh, that, well she is someone you don't need to worry about," she tells me as she makes her way over to the woman in the grand hallway.

Frankie's smile is sinister as she reaches her. "Ah, I see someone ordered a cunt." Her lips tip up in a scowl, and I suck my bottom lip in, holding back laughter at what Frankie just said.

The shocked expression on her face is priceless, even if she looks like she stepped off the cover of *Vogue*.

She looks down at Frankie with disgust. "I see Nico still hasn't got you under control," she sneers. "I am here for Gabe. We have a session."

"Why are you here when we're coming downtown to you?" I blurt out.

"Let's just say Gabe is a special case, and well..." She looks down at her claw-like nails, sucking in her bottom lip. "He and I, we have something, so I am here to discuss where we go from here, not that it is any of your business. We have discussed this in your sessions, Rosie, you want to know too much," she accuses.

Who the hell does she think she is? I didn't want to go to her sessions, and we hardly speak at them anyway. I have only gone to keep Nico and Gabe happy. Inhaling deeply, I pull my arm away from Frankie and head toward the room I have shared with Gabe for the last six months and push the door open.

"You have a visitor." I look at him, my jaw clenching as I didn't expect this to be as hard as it is.

"Angel, what's wrong, who is it?" he asks, sitting forward and stretching out his arm, trying to reach for me, only this time I don't go to him.

"It's Sophia, our therapist." My tone is bitter as I meet his eyes, and any of the sparkle I have when I look at him is gone. It's like looking at a stranger. That's when I hear the clicking of heels across the floor heading toward the room, and the sinking feeling inside makes me feel sick.

"Oh, baby, I have finally done it. I told my boss I can't work with you anymore, that we have a relationship building between us." She barges past me and lunges at him.

"What are you talking about?" He leans back to escape her grasp, but I have seen the way he looks at her when he thinks I am not looking.

I smile sweetly at them as I clear my throat. "I won't be here after today, but as I promised Nico, I will continue my appointments with you." Dipping my head, I make my way out of the room, not looking back.

"Wait, Angel, where are you going?" I hear Gabe calling me as I leave, but I can't turn back. I know he has me here because he feels like he owes me for getting him out of the basement after we were kidnapped by O'Conner.

Sometimes I wish I were back there, just the two of us in the basement, chained to the walls, metal digging into my wrists. It was awful, and I wasn't there for as long as him, but he was with me the whole time. Every day he was with me, even if we didn't speak, and even when I was taken advantage of, he stayed by my side, giving me the courage I needed to survive. He's given me the courage I need to do what I am doing now, even if he doesn't realize it.

"What the fuck was that?" Frankie says.

"We need to leave," I tell her. "I also need to find somewhere to stay while I sort my crap out." I look at her and smile.

Shaking her head, she smiles. "You can stay at my old place. I am mostly here anyway."

"That's great. I need to get myself back and show everyone they can't walk over me. I am tired of being the kind Rosie who sits in the corner. I have been running away from things that I need to face and have responsibilities I need to deal with." I take hold of Frankie's shoulder, mimicking her. Inhaling deeply and realizing what I have ahead of me. "And you're just the person to help me do it." If anyone can help me, she is the only one I know that can.

"Fuck yeah," she hollers. She laughs as we walk out of the big oak doors, pulling me close. "You've got this, Rose."

Chapter 2

Gabe

What the fuck is happening? Everything was fine this morning when I woke up, then suddenly, she's leaving.

"Sophia, what are you talking about? There isn't anything between us." I start to get out of bed, but she pushes me back down, wedging herself on the bed next to me.

"What do you mean? I know you want me. We have a connection between us; I can feel it. We are meant to be together." Her fake plumped lips make their way to mine, and my senses are overwhelmed with her perfume. Fuck knows what it is, but I can't fucking breathe.

Shoving her away, I get out of the bed on the other side, standing only in my boxer briefs and watch as she looks at me in disbelief.

"We're it for each other Gabe, what's going on?" I can see the confusion written all over her face.

Maybe she is the one who needs to see a therapist because I have literally no idea what I have done to give this woman the impression I want her in any way. My eyes are on one woman only, and she has just walked out the fucking door.

"Look, Sophia, I am sorry if you got the wrong impression, but you and me." I gesture between us. "We are not a thing, nor will we ever be." My head turns to the door automatically, and I feel her eyes follow my movements.

"N-n-no," she stutters. "You can't want that street rat over me!" Rage fills her features.

"Watch your mouth," I warn, my jaw clenching at her disrespect of my angel.

"You can't be serious, look at me!" she shouts. "What man doesn't want a woman like me?" Her head tilts to the side as her lips pucker, as if she is trying to tempt me.

"This man. Now get the fuck out before I am forced to make you." I point toward the door. I can't believe this woman. How can someone be so arrogant?

With a huff, she turns and heads out the door, stopping just before exiting. "We are meant to be, you will see, even if I have to make you." Her golden locks are tossed over her shoulder, her heels click as she leaves.

Sighing heavily, I drop onto the bed, it squeaks in protest. Reaching into the drawer, I pick up my phone, finding who I am looking for, I hit call.

"Nico, I have a problem," I tell him before he even speaks.

"I'm on my way," he tells me before I can elaborate.

"Wait, when I say problem, I mean the kind that's about 5ft, blonde and smells like she's bathed in a perfume bottle." I pinch the bridge of my nose between my thumb and forefinger.

He laughs deeply down the line. "What the fuck! You're serious?" he asks. "*Fratello*, you don't waste any time. When we last spoke, you were fawning over Rosie, what have I missed?"

"Two things, motherfucker! One, I wasn't fawning over anyone, and second, she's gone." I bang my fist on the bedside table, trying to control my annoyance at my brother not taking this shit seriously.

"Gabe, look, calm down, and tell me what the problem is?" he soothes.

"That quack you set us up with is adamant we belong together, and now Rosie thinks something is going on between us and has left...with Frankie," I sneer.

"Watch it, Gabe, there will be a fucking good reason why Frankie left with her, and as for the quack, you needed to speak to someone, you've been through a lot. You were held hostage for two years, for fuck's sake! I did what anyone else would do, and she came highly recommended by the doctor," he tells me frankly.

As if I have fucking forgotten what that fucker O'Connor did to me, and trust me, the mood I am in right now, he is gonna wish Nico didn't leave his life in my fucking hands. I dismiss those thoughts as I don't want Nico to think he has to worry about me, as that's all he seems to be doing.

"Well, you need to get hold of her to see what's going on. Rosie needs to get back here, and as for that doctor, you need to get us a new one." I sound like a sulky fucker, but I am annoyed Rosie didn't even hear me out, she just left at the word of some woman we see on a weekly basis. I mean, what about the time we've spent together... Do I really not mean anything to her at all?

"I'll speak to her," he tells me and ends the call.

Great, now what the fuck am I supposed to do? I know one thing for sure, I need to keep an eye on Sophia. Fuck knows what she meant, but I didn't like her tone.

I make my way out of the room and head through the hallways filled with our childhood memories. I have no idea why Nico didn't change any of this when he took over, but it all feels odd being here knowing my father isn't. I get an eerie feeling. This place needs to change, to look more like my brother owns it and not like a museum.

"Gabe." I turn as I hear Tony call my name.

"Hey, man, how are you doing? Your leg looks like it's getting better." I chuckle as I watch him hobble over to me using the walking aid he despises.

"Fuck you! I'm getting enough shit for this as it is, without getting anymore from you," he hisses.

I laugh as I turn and walk away, knowing full well he will have to hobble faster to catch up with me. I hear him mutter and curse as the tapping of his stick gets faster and faster.

"Hey, listen, I need you to run me over to the gym. I want to get back into the office. I am sick of looking at the same four walls," he grumbles.

"And that pretty nurse isn't helping the view," I say as I turn around, raising my brow in question.

"It's not like that, man. Come on, stop giving me shit. I want to get back to normal. I need to get back to the gym." He falls into one of the occasion chairs in the hallway, his aid crashing to the floor as his head drops into his hands.

"You know I never meant for any of this to happen. I didn't even know Nico was fucking Frankie. Sure, she's hot, but that was all it was for me. I know I lied about her being a female, but I didn't realize he would find out the way he did." His eyes meet mine, and I can see how sincere he is. "Look, we've known each other a long time, and how often have you ever known your brother to watch a kill go down? He always sends one of the guys unless he plans to do it himself."

"I know, man, but the point is...were you ever gonna tell him? It's the fact that you kept this from him. We're family, we don't keep shit from each other. Sure, you may have got your ass kicked for lying, but if you'd told him from the start, you could have prevented any of this from happening at all." I shake my head. I can't believe Tony, of all people, would have kept something from any of us. He even kept it from Marco—his own brother. Would I have shot him and made him fuck my woman in front of me like Nico did...maybe not. I may be a crazy motherfucker, but Nico is a level up from us all, and Tony knows that. He was lucky to come away with a bullet in his leg and not his head.

"Look, you need to stop wallowing in the past and concentrate on the future. Nico probably did you a favor." I smile at him as I watch his eyes bug out of his head. "Look at it this way, if he hadn't shot you, you wouldn't have the pretty little nurse giving you bed baths every day, which I am almost certain you don't need anymore." This time I turn and leave him, only calling back to let him know that we will head to the gym once I have showered and changed.

I need to vent and think of a way to get my angel back, and sort this shit out with Sophia.

CHAPTER 3

Rosie

A FEW WEEKS LATER

"Motherfucker!" I shout to no one in particular, but I hear Frankie laugh as she approaches me.

"I knew I would hear those sweet words come from your pretty little mouth sooner or later." She grips my shoulders from behind and whispers in my ear, "That's it, imagine that punch bag is him, or her, whoever you fancy, but whoever you imagine, give them fucking hell."

She isn't wrong. For the last few weeks, I have been slipping back into bad habits, and I have been paying for it at night. The nightmares plague me, making me cranky and suspicious of everyone. My paranoia is through the roof, and I am sure I am being watched.

Each time I hit the red and white bag hanging from the ceiling, it's not Gabe or Sophia I am thinking of, but Ms.

Dunn, the woman who plagues my dreams, the woman who made my childhood worse than it needed to be.

When my mother died...I stop and laugh to myself as I pull the bag close, hugging it as I let myself go back to the day we parted. I have tried over and over to just say she died, but each time I do, the memory of her dead eyes looking at me, arm outstretched and reaching for me, plays over and over like a movie on repeat. That's when my life went downhill, that moment right there. The man responsible, I can still see his dark brown eyes and hear his voice threatening that if I ever spoke of this night again, then he would make sure I end up the same way as my mother. And I didn't speak for years, which is why I almost aged out of the system, but not until Ms. Dunn got me speaking again, and of course a lady should never swear. The moment I did, it would be a beating and my mouth washed out with soap, and not to forget "time to reflect" in the basement...alone.

If it weren't for Harridan, I would never have made it there. She saved my life more than once, and we had plans, big ones. We were gonna get out, make something of ourselves, only I didn't. That's when my stepfather decided to make an appearance.

"Hey, heads up, Gabe is on his way," Frankie calls over. "Tony wants to come and look at the books or some shit." Her shoulders shrug as she picks up the towels and tosses them into the basket in the corner.

"Thanks, I am heading out. I have stuff to do," I tell her as I unstrap the tape from my knuckles, scrunch it up into a ball and throw it into the bin. I swig some water and head toward the door and bump into a wall of perfume.

"Sorry, honey, I didn't see you there." Her golden locks are pulled high in a ponytail on top of her head, her

Lycra leggings and sports bra show that she visits the gym way more than I do.

"It's fine," I tell her as I move to go around her, trying to ignore the smarmy look she is giving me. I know what she is thinking...I have him, and you want him.

"Oh, is Gabe here yet, we're meeting here." She smiles as she applies lip gloss to her plump pink lips.

I mean, who wears lip gloss at the gym?

"I couldn't tell you. I wasn't looking for him. You'll have to check with Frankie in the office." I shrug.

The purr of an engine catches both of our attention, and I hear her giggle. It makes me want to puke, especially when I see who is in the car. Fucking hell, it's him. I increase my pace and look straight ahead, but I don't get far as he stops the car and jumps out of the driver's side.

"Angel." He catches up with me, grabbing my arm and turning me to him. Sophia has started to make her way over, calling him, but he hasn't acknowledged her, which is odd.

"Fuck off, Gabe, leave me alone. Sophia wants you," I tell him, pulling my arm away. He frowns at me, and I know why; he is surprised at my attitude. In fact, I am not sure he has ever seen me this way before.

I hear him growl as he turns to Sophia and tells her to back off, then calls out to me, "You're mine, angel." His brow arches as he looks deep into my eyes. "I will make you understand that."

I roll my eyes at him and turn my back as he and Sophia start to bicker like they've been together for years. I don't know why he continues to try to contact me. He clearly has something going on with her, and if what she says is true, they are engaged to be married. Right now, I don't have time for this crap, I have bigger things to worry about... Like who is following me. If I am right, then I have to get rid of them. I closed that chapter a long time ago, and I don't want to go back. It's called the past for a reason, and I don't think I could relive it.

New York was a fresh start for me, and if it wasn't for O'Connor, I would still be working the bar in his club, minding my own business, but for some unknown reason, which he never did enlighten me on, he thought I was stealing from him...which was nonsense. I am not a thief. I have done a lot in my time, bad things, things I am not proud of, but stealing is not one of those things. There has to be more to it than that. The only way to know why is to ask him, but as he is tied up in a container somewhere, that would be hard to do.

"What the hell!" I start to scream, but a hand covers my mouth as I am dragged down an alleyway and pushed up against the wall. I try to use the techniques I have been working on with Frankie, but the grip they have on me is too tight, then I look up and my body relaxes.

"Are you guys serious? What do you think you are doing?" I yell. I can't believe who I am looking at. I ran from them just over two years ago and never wanted to look back.

"Hey, boss," Massimo says as he loosens his grip on me.

My face scrunches as I look between both him and Enzo. Boss? What are they talking about?

"What? Why are you here?" I ask, confusion written all over my face. "And why have you been following me, because it is you that's been following me right?"

"We've been trying to track you since you left. Everyone thought you'd been kidnapped by the Blanco family." His head rises to the sky. "After what they did to Theo, we couldn't bear to think what they could be doing to you, but when we stormed their homes and couldn't locate you, we didn't know what to think." His hands take my face as if he can't believe I'm alive.

"We took each member one by one, but no one said anything. The ones who did speak, said they knew nothing and swore they had nothing to do with the death of Theo or your disappearance, but we knew they were lying." He pulls me close, hugging me tightly.

"You should know we lost a lot of men fighting to find you and avenge the death of your father," he tells me, pulling back and smiling, looking deep into my eyes, which are burning from the tears I can fill building but don't want to spill. The tears are not for Theo, that man got what he deserved, but not from the Blanco family...from me, and if they find out what I did, I will be dead too.

"You have to come back. We have started to recruit, but you are La Madrina now. I can't lie, there is unrest as the men need to see we have a leader, Rosie, and Theo's wish was for it to be you."

"What? That doesn't happen. Why can't it be you? You were his second in command, why can't you step up?" I ramble. I can't believe Theo would do this! I should have known that son of a bitch would keep me tied to him somehow, but to take his place is ridiculous.

That bastard killed my mother, right in front of me, and threatened me with the same fate if I said a word, then threw me into a children's home for years to go through hell until he was ready to have me back... until he was ready to use me as leverage in his business deals. He thought I would forget his voice, but I knew it was him as soon as I heard it.

I let him believe I was happy he returned for me, fooling everyone I wanted to be back, but in reality, I was biding my time until I could get him alone. Karma really is a bitch, and it turns out not only for him but also for me too.

The night I ran from there and got on the back of Harridan's motorbike, I thought I was free. We had the time of our lives, and she tried to persuade me to go with her, but I knew we had to separate, we couldn't be connected. I assumed the first place people would look would be my only connections, but they went for the trap of the Blanco family instead. All it took was a couple of fake emails for them to follow and that is apparently all it takes to start a war between families.

"I can't come back. I have a life here." Well, sort of anyway, but they don't need to know that.

"Rosie, you don't have a choice. We're here to take you, you have to come back, you have to fulfill your responsibilities. Too many people are relying on you." He inhales deeply, and I watch as he works his jaw. "Please, Rosie, don't make us take you by force."

I look to the sky as I close my eyes, feeling the anger building inside of me at Theo still having a hold even from his grave.

"Look, give me a week, and I will come back. I have things I need to sort out here."

"Fine, one week and then we head back to New Jersey." He nods in agreement.

CHAPTER 4

Rosie

I AM WELL AND truly screwed, and there is only one person that can help me right now, but can I call them after all this time? I just don't think I have any other option, she's my ride or die, and she will know what to do. Before I can talk myself out of it, my phone is out of my pocket, and I am dialing the number I memorized. It doesn't ring long before the familiar voice comes through the receiver.

"Well, fuck me, babe, it's been a minute."

I realize I was tense as my shoulders relax at the smile I hear in her voice. "Hey, H, how are you?" I ask, and I don't think she will ever truly know how much I have missed her. We spent every day together in the children's home, and we planned our lives together until I was taken out...by him and then of course, like usual when I needed her on the night things took a turn, she was there to take me to safety.

Sure, New York and New Jersey are not far, but in all honestly, who is gonna look right under their nose, and I was right. It took them almost two years to locate me, and if all this crap with O'Connor hadn't happened, I am not sure I would still be here. I had gotten friendly with some of the other staff who were talking about heading west, it sounded fun. So, who knows what could have gone down for me, but now here I am, on the phone with the one person who I trust the most in the whole world, needing her help once again.

"I'm good, but I am guessing you not so much, otherwise you wouldn't be calling, right? Let me guess, they caught up with you?" she says as she starts shuffling things around in the background.

"Yep, you guessed it. I am sorry to bring you into this, but I have no one else," I confess.

She chuckles. "Babe, I live for this shit. Where are you? We can meet and go through what's happening." I give her my address, and she cackles. "You're shitting me, you live in that shithole?"

"Hey, there is nothing wrong with where I live, the people around here are lovely." I am a little offended, but I do know what she means. Frankie's place is in a run-down part of town, and where I lived before was far from that.

"Settle down, princess, and meet me in the café on the corner of West Fifty-Sixth Street, in an hour," she tells me and cuts the line.

I sigh in relief, as she will be able to help clear up one part of my shitty life. I will just need to sort out the rest.

I have time for a shower before I need to meet her, but I should really stop and get some cat food at the store. I appear to have adopted a couple of stray cats. Frankie is gonna kill me if she finds out, but I can't just let them go hungry, plus, they're company considering I don't do anything in the evenings aside from thinking about him. As if that wasn't enough of a headache, now I have this shitstorm brewing.

I hear the jingle of the bell as I enter the store and pick up my groceries. Glancing out the window, I notice Sophia on the corner, and it's like she is trying to hide, but in a really bad way. What the hell is she trying to do...follow me? Why?

Grabbing my bag, I head home but take a detour. Lifting my phone and reversing the camera, I notice she is still on my tail. Fucking hell, this isn't what I need right now. I figure she will know where Frankie lives, so I might as well stop the longest walk home and let her see me go in, if that is her plan, and find out what she does from there.

Firing off a text to Frankie, I let her know I am being followed by Sophia and send the image of her behind me. My phone starts to ring instantly.

"What the fuck? How long has that twunt been following you?"

"I noticed her when I was in the store getting cat food?" If I drop that in now, she will never notice.

"And you did a detour to make sure she was actually following you?" she questions.

"Of course," I tell her as I place the paper bag on the floor to get my keys from my gym bag.

"Where is she now?" I hear the anger in her voice as she starts to pace the room, her footsteps heavy as she stomps around the office at the gym.

I look over my shoulder and snigger.

"What's fucking funny?" she spits out.

"She's standing across the street on the sidewalk, looking at the sign on the post. She really isn't very good at this." I get the keys and enter the main building, hearing the click of the door as it shuts behind me, leaving Sophia outside, oblivious to the fact I am aware of her following me.

"Oh, and you know the lift is still broken, and the door is still jammed?" I grumble as I walk up the stairs, balancing the phone on my shoulder, pressing my ear against it, and my gym bag and shopping in the other arm, the keys dangling in my hand as I approach the front entrance. I jiggle the key in the lock and shove my shoulder into the door, forcing it open, and I almost follow through and fall on my ass.

"See, did you hear that? This door is lethal!" I moan as I toss the keys on the table to the left of the door, closing the door with my foot.

I discard my gym bag on the floor and carry the grocery bag into the kitchen and place it on the side as I spy the cats lurking at the window and smile, thinking I got away with it.

"Cat food, why would you need to stop off for cat food, you don't have a cat?" she quizzes me.

"Erm, well it's a funny story, and we didn't have but kinda have two now," I rush out. "Anyway, is there anything you can do to keep Sophia away from me? I have some things I need to sort out, and I really could do without her being on my case right now. I don't even know what she wants with me," I groan. "She's got the guy, isn't that enough?" I sound like a child throwing a tantrum, but seriously, that woman has it all, yet she wants to follow me around...why? To rub it in.

"I will get Nico to get one of the guys on it, persuade her to move on, shall we say." I hear the smile in her voice. "Oh, and get rid of those fucking cats!" The line goes dead before I can respond.

If she thinks I am getting rid of them, she has another think coming.

CHAPTER 5

Gabe

SEEING SOPHIA AT THE gym today has really fucked me off. I don't know how many times I have to tell this woman there is fuck-all between us, but she clearly isn't getting the memo. Of course, to make things fucking worse, Rosie was there to see her, which now makes her believe we are an item, but she will be mine no matter what I have to do to make her see it.

I stomp over to the office as I see Tony on the phone in there, lifting my head in acknowledgment, and he looks up at me as I enter, putting the phone down.

"Remind me to get an Uber next time. Traveling with you is too much fucking drama, man, and that's shit I don't want to get involved in. You and your brother attract crazy fucking women." He shakes his head as he leans back in his swirly office chair.

"What's happened?" I question and sit opposite him. The office looks different, and he looks out of place.

The papers on his desk are all in order, and you can see someone else has been in here. This is not the way Tony runs things, it's too...orderly, and it's fucking with his head.

"What's happened, are you shitting me? Your brother, my cousin, shot me in the fucking leg and made me fuck his fucking woman in front of him, Gabe. That shit is fucked up, and to top it all off, he let her take over the gym while I was recovering. Look what she's done to the place while I've been away." He throws his arm around the office at the neatly lined papers.

"I am not sure this is for me anymore. I know what I did was wrong, but I didn't fuck her knowing they were together. We're family, man." He runs his hands over his shaved head.

"Look, take a minute and think things through. You're back now, and the gym is yours to run how you want, Frankie knows that. We all do. The past is the past, and we all need to move on, including you." I look at him pointedly.

The phone on his desk rings, cutting off our conversation, and he picks it up and looks at me as the person on the other end speaks.

"You got it, boss," he responds.

So, Nico is giving him a job...interesting. I knew he couldn't leave him out of the fold for long. Tony is a good capo, one you can't do without, and from what I know about what went down, this really is about Nico being a jealous motherfucker. Would I tell him that? Sure, but is it worth the conversion? Absolutely fucking not.

"What is it?" I ask.

"Sophia," is all he says.

I stand up from the chair and rest my knuckles on the desk. "What about her?"

"Rosie called Frankie, Sophia's been following her and is outside her apartment. He wants someone to move her on," he tells me as he reaches for his aid and stands.

"Where are you going?" I walk toward him.

"To get one of the guys over there and suggest she move on, like I was told." He shrugs.

"Leave it with me," I tell him as I leave his office and head through the gym, the music beating in time with my heart. I can hear him calling me, and I know this isn't a good idea, but I am all out of fucks now. Sophia has run out of chances with me.

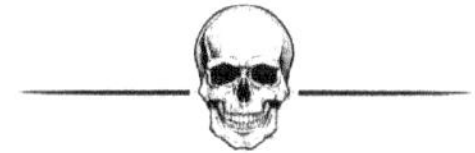

I park a few blocks away and walk the rest, keeping my eye out for Sophia but don't see her anywhere. She must have decided she had seen enough for today, but I hung around for a while just to make sure she didn't return.

I must be there about an hour before Rosie leaves her apartment, dressed in cut-off denim shorts and a baseball T-shirt, her hair pulled back in a ponytail. She looks fucking stunning. Unable to help myself, I have to know where she is going, who would she be meeting? Frankie will be with Nico now, and as she spent most of her time with me the past few months, I haven't heard her mention any friends that she would now be meeting with.

I get to the corner and watch as she disappears into a café. Shit, I can't follow her in there without getting spotted, so I stay out here and see who she's meeting. I watch as she looks around, searching for whoever she is meeting, and hear the rumble of a motorbike stop outside the café. She smiles so brightly it lights up her whole face, and I want to kill the motherfucker on the bike. I want to be the only person to make her smile like that. Who is he?

They kick the stand down and pull off their helmet, long brown locks fall down their back. This is not a he, it's a she. What the fuck is happening, and who is that?

Rosie comes running out of the café, and they hug each other like they haven't seen each other in years. The woman on the bike quickly adjusts herself, as if showing any kind of emotion is an odd sensation for her. I chuckle to myself because she reminds me of Frankie. Rosie links arms with her, and they go inside, sitting at a table near the window. I want to get a closer look as I see some kind of patch on the bike, but it's too far away. I can't get closer because she will see me, but what the fuck is Rosie doing meeting up with someone from a motorcycle club? I pull my phone from my pocket and fire off a text to Tony.

Gabe: I need a list of all the MCs around here.

Tony: Why?

Gabe: Curious.

Tony: Sure you are.

Gabe: Just do it.

Tony: On it.

In the meantime, I am gonna have to wait until he gets back to me. If she is in trouble, I need to know about it.

CHAPTER 6

Rosie

I HEAR HARRIDAN BEFORE I see her, and I jump up out of my seat and run outside. Seeing her is like being at home. I have missed her so much. She is the sister I never had, and I watch as she gets off her bike, such a badass. She shakes her hair out like a model and makes it look effortless. I know she isn't one for affection, but I can't help myself. I wrap my arms around her and pull her close. I feel her embrace me, then she pulls back.

"Okay, that's enough PDA, let's head inside," she tells me with a smile, and I link our arms and head back inside to the table near the window.

"Are you sure you want to sit near the window?" she asks.

"Why not?" I look over at her with a smile. "I know I am being followed either by Sophia, the Contis, and I wouldn't put it past Gabe. You know my life has been crazy." I shake my head and rub both my eyes with my finger and thumb.

"Girl, are you crazy, this is fucking exciting." She jumps a little in her seat. "Right, so break this shit down for me as I need to catch up." She claps. "Tell me, Gabe is the hot guy you were kidnapped with, right?" she smirks.

"Kinda and being kidnapped isn't a good thing." I shake my head at her.

"Well, that depends on who is doing the kidnapping." She winks.

"Jesus!" I laugh. "Look, I worked for O'Connor in a bar, and he thought I was stealing from him. So, he basically put me in his basement, and Gabe was also down there." I look down as I remember what happened with O'Connor.

"What, what's wrong?" She reaches over and touches my hand.

"Nothing. Look, let's just say O'Connor wasn't a pleasant host, and he did things I didn't want to, okay." I pull my hand back and pick up the menu, pretending to look at it.

She snatches it from my hand. "So, what you're saying is priority one, cut his balls off and make him eat them?" She pulls a tooth pick out from the holder on the table and starts to tap it on the table.

"He is being dealt with, so we can't get hung up on him. We have other issues we need to concentrate on." I cover my hands.

She frowns at me. "Other priorities? Hon, that won't take long, trust me, it's a five-minute job."

"I know you can sort this, but, H, we need to sort out my other issues." I nod, trying to reassure her.

"Fine, shoot." She nods.

"Theo Conti. You know what happened, well, you also know he left me in charge." I look up to the ceiling and watch the fan as it spins over and over, kinda how my brain is right now. "Apparently, I am La Madrina and have to go back to New Jersey. Massimo and Enzo have allowed me a week." I study my nails as if they have the answer to what I will do next.

"Okay, and what's the issue with that? New Jersey isn't that far away, and you'll be closer to me." She smiles brightly. "And, hey, you're gonna be boss lady." She snorts out a laugh. "You know how unheard of that is. You should grab this with both hands and run with it," she tells me.

"I get all that, H, I really do, but running New Jersey, me?" I point to myself and laugh.

"Yeah, hon, you, and why the fuck not? After all the shit you've been through, you deserve this." She raises her arm up to call a waitress. "How long does it take to get service around here?"

The waitress comes over, and we order our drinks, just sitting in silence as I think about what she said. Sure, I can do it, but that would mean I have to be present in New Jersey. I couldn't be here in New York every day. My mind keeps going back to Gabe and the time we spent with each other. Was it all in my head, the feelings, was it all only on my side?

"Look, whatever is stopping you from taking this opportunity, you have to shut it down. You know why Theo did this, he thought you'd fail and his men would disobey you." She takes a sip of her coffee, which the waitress delivered a few moments ago, and smiles above the rim. "It appears his wishes have not been granted, La Madrina, his men are welcoming you into the fold. They started a war for you, embrace it." She places her mug back on the table with force, spilling some of the contents on to the table, and we laugh at the unbelievable situation.

"What's your other situation, because from what I see, you have to pack up and move back, no issues."

"Gabe," I say and look out the window as I watch people walk up and down on the sidewalk.

"Ah, the man you have fallen for?" Her eyes roll as she tuts loudly and places her hand on her chest.

"I haven't fallen for him, I just..." I start.

"Just what, babe? You want to jump his bones otherwise he wouldn't be an issue." She smirks.

"It's not only him. He has a fiancé," I sneer. "One who also happens to be following me," I huff.

"Ooh, exciting." She begins to clap again. "So, we can kidnap her and cut off her tits and feed them to her?" Her brows raise in question.

"What, no!" I frown and shake my head. "What's wrong with you?" I ask.

"Nothing is wrong with me. I see a problem, and I am just eliminating it. What's your plan for the skank?" She lifts her mug and finishes her coffee.

"I don't know. I think leaving will be enough."

"Leaving is never enough, you should have learned that by now, but it's your call." She sighs. "So, what is the plan?"

"I am gonna pack up and leave, but I need to make sure she doesn't follow, the same goes for anyone else. No one can know where I am going until I decide the time is right," I tell her.

"You got it. I will make sure you get back without being followed," she tells me.

The rest of our catch up is in silence. I know she doesn't agree with what I want to do, but I feel leaving in silence is the best all round. I can sort out everything from New Jersey.

It's not like anyone will miss me.

CHAPTER 7

Gabe

I SLIDE OPEN THE container door, and it crashes against the wall, bringing everyone's attention to me.

"Everyone, disappear." I look around at the men staring back at me. "Now!"

Heading toward Tony's office I watch as Nico appears. "What did you call him for?" I look over at Tony, ignoring my brother.

"He didn't, but he should have." Nico eyes Tony but doesn't say anything else. He smoothly perches on the desk and looks me dead in the eye. "What do you want with the Soul Reapers?"

"Who?" I raise my brow.

"The MC, why are you looking into them? We don't want any trouble, Gabe. They're a solid club, and we have always been on good terms, so what's going on?" He stands and walks over to me. "I want the truth," he demands, face-to-face with me.

Tony stands and excuses himself from the office, closing the door behind him.

"Why go to Tony to get information when you could have asked me? You know if something's wrong I have your back, brother." He looks disappointed.

"This is personal, and I can take care of it myself. It isn't anything worth worrying about until I know what I'm dealing with." I walk around him and take Tony's seat.

"And...what are you dealing with?" He turns, waiting for my response.

"Rosie met up with some chick from an MC. I couldn't see which one, as I was too far away, so I got Tony to look at all the local ones." I spin in the chair and see the desk is in chaos. It appears Tony is getting himself settled back in.

"There is only one MC local, *fratello*, and that's the Soul Reapers, you should know that. What's gotten into you?" He looks at me in disbelief.

I don't know what to tell him. If I was thinking clearly, I wouldn't have texted Tony. I know the only main MC around here, and no others would cross paths without them knowing, but I was too blinded by anger to even think to reach out and ask what their connection is. Shank, their Prez, is a reasonable guy and would have spoken to me, but now Nico is involved.

"You're right, I wasn't thinking. I am still getting back on my feet, and all this shit with Sophia is getting to me. Honestly, I lost my shit when I heard she was following Rosie." I open the filing cabinet behind me and pull out Tony's secret bottle of vodka and two glasses, placing them in front of Nico.He nods in agreement, and I can see he understands where I am coming from. I know I shouldn't be sending out feelers on the MC, and I was lucky I only asked Tony otherwise we could have a mob of bikers coming over the bridge, getting in our business, and that's not what we need right now. Nico is right, we have existed side by side without issues, so we need to make sure it stays that way.

"I understand. I will contact Shank and ask why someone from his club was meeting with Rosie and see what he knows," he says. He lifts his glass in salut. "You know he may keep his cards close to his chest for now, they protect their own...just like we do," he tells me.

"I know, but asking may rattle some cages, it may make her come to me." I shrug. "Even if she's pissed, she'll be talking to me, and that's a start." I toss my drink back in one gulp.

Nico laughs and follows my lead. "What would we do without them?" He smiles, and I see the twinkle in his eye. I have never seen my brother like this before, but it suits him. Frankie is good for him. They're both crazy...and not just for each other.

Blowing out a breath, I look at Nico and smile. "I have some business to take care of at the yard, let me know what you hear from Shank."

He stands and walks over to me, pulling me toward him in a half hug and pats my back. "I'm proud of you, *fratello*."

Tapping his back, I nod. "It's time, I have to move forward," I tell him as I break away from him and leave the office. Turning back to speak to him, he tells me, "I will let you know." Nodding, I leave without another word.

My mind's spinning as I pull up to the gates and see Tommy as I arrived. Nico obviously called ahead to tell him I was coming. He hasn't changed...well, he's aged, but the lucky fucker has aged like a fine wine. He always did have women falling over themselves for him, but he doesn't seem interested, and I suspect that's because of this bookshop owner he's been trying to keep to himself. He thinks we don't know about her, but he's not been doing a very good job of hiding it.

I lift my finger on the soft leather wheel of my Audi R8 as I cruise through the open gates and press the button to open the window to greet him.

"What's up man?" I nod.

"What's up?" He returns my nod.

"Today's the day. I assume everything I need is in there?" I smile but I'm far from being happy.

"Sure is, and we've left him for a few days. Apart from the basic rations he's not seen anyone," he informs me, which is good to hear.

I haven't seen this mother fucker since I closed my eyes the last time he drugged me. And those memories are the ones that play on repeat, and that's exactly what he's going to pay for.

O'Connor will pay and today is when Karma comes and bites this son of a bitch in the ass.

Driving around to the container he has been kept in for the last six months, I get out of my car and close the door behind me. Shrugging off my suit jacket I toss it through the open window and head toward the rusty blue cell that's been his nightmare. If he thinks what he put me through was bad, he hasn't seen anything yet.

CHAPTER 8

Gabe

THE DOOR OPENS WITH a squeak that is enough to raise the hairs on anyone's neck, but for most that end up in here, they know they won't be leaving alive. Each time these doors open, I know they must be questioning if today is the day.

I slam the door behind me, just to hear it clatter against the metal and watch O'Connor jump at my arrival. It smells of piss, shit, and something else I can't quite put my finger on but is making my nose twitch.

I hadn't realized how much I missed this, not until this moment right here, watching him sit in the middle of the container with the single light swaying above his head, casting shadows along the side of the walls. I can see him trying to work out who is here to see him, but he can't turn his head far enough around. I know he won't say anything, not yet anyway. If he is anything like the others I have had in here, then he will do one of two things. He will believe an apology will set him free or try to negotiate with me. Unfortunately for him, neither will work.

I lean in close enough he can feel my warm breath on his cold skin, but I don't touch him. Not touching is worse. Every nerve in his body is screaming, waiting for the moment contact comes. The waiting stretches longer than any pain I inflict ever could.

"You're imagining what I'll do," I whisper. "And the truth is, your imagination will be crueler than I will ever need to be."

Rule number one. Fear breeds in silence.

I step back into the corner of the room and simply watch. Minutes pass. His breathing grows ragged, shallow. He is breaking himself faster than I could. Faster than usual but I have to remember he has already been here six months and been tortured by our men. That is usually the secret. The body can resist blows. But the mind? The mind destroys itself, given the right push. This is all still true, but they have made this easier for me.

Usually, that is exactly what I would do, play with their minds, but as I stand watching him, I remember what he did, and not just to me but to her...Rosie. Anger rises inside me like a ball of flames burning from the inside trying to get out.

That's why when I move toward him and knock him off his chair with one punch, he doesn't see it coming, just the blur of movement, but I don't miss the explosion of pain that makes his face scrunch and the grunt as the air is knocked from his lungs. His body lays limp on the floor, all fight lost, which is a little disappointing, but I knew this would be the case, he has been here too long. I should know better than anyone that being in confinement takes its toll and after a certain time you just lose all your fight. Unless you find someone in there with you that makes you want to live.

Unluckily for O'Conner, we do not usually put people together unless it benefits us.

Bending down, I grab his neck, jerking him upright, feeling his cold skin against mine as I lean in close to his ear. "Missed me?" I whisper calmly.

Blood from his nose runs down to his mouth and drips off his chin as I watch tears start to fall. I am impressed; the men here have certainly done a number on him. I release my grip on his neck and toss him to the floor, collapsing as he starts to cough and splutter, blood covering his naked chest. He looks up at me and that's when I get it—iron, that's the other smell. Fuck, I knew I'd smelled it before. Smells fucking good.

Moving closer, I hover above him. Up close one of his eyes is swollen shut, the other is looking frantically around, almost as if part of him believes there may be a way to get out still. He shivers from the slight chill in the air. They have been coming in and out leaving him in different states of dress to mess with his mind, and I got him in boxers.

"Get back in the chair," I order and watch as he scrambles to follow my instructions without hesitation.

I leave him to it as I make my way to the side where cabinets with everything you could ever dream of waiting for me. A torturer's heaven. I don't know what goes on in Tommy's mind when I open the cabinets one by one to inspect what's there, but I smile when I see what I want and place them on the silver surgical trolley next to the cabinets and wheel it over toward my very special guest.

I circle him, running my hand across the back of the chair lightly. Pulling the cuffs from the back of my pants I bend and secure him to the chair. The smallest sound in the container grows tenfold. I watch his breathing get heavier as I do nothing else but circle him and watch like he is my prey and I am on the hunt, waiting for the right time to pounce.

There is nothing I would love more than to beat the living shit out of O'Connor, but he deserves something much more than that for what he put Rosie through, and I think I know what that is and just how to do it.

We all know pain is fleeting. But anticipation? That's endless. And tonight, I intend to let him drown in it.

CHAPTER 9

Rosie

THE PING FROM MY phone tells me it's time for me to head out, but I can't find Meow, and I know she hasn't eaten today. I should be clearing out, but I need to know she has at least eaten before I go. I can't take them with me no matter how much I want to. Another ping and know I have to go. I don't have time to hang around, so I pick up the one bag I have and head through the door, taking one last look around the small apartment I have been staying in. I really enjoyed it here, my own space.

I know my life is going to be changed forever. I know I am going to have to head back no matter what, but I can't go back directly just in case that crazy bitch is still following me.

My phone is going off again, so I decide I should probably check it in case something has happened I need to know about.

Frankie: Hey, bitch, call me

Frankie: Why the fuck are you ignoring me?
Frankie: You need to call me NOW!

I lean against the wall in the hallway and sigh. I shouldn't leave her hanging, she has helped me, and I need to let her know I am okay. Scrolling to her number I press the call button, and it barely rings once before she answers.

"Finally, why the fuck haven't you been answering me?" she blurts out, a hint of panic in her voice.

I feel bad that I have hardly contacted her, especially after I told her I was being followed.

"Frankie, I am sorry. I have had a lot going on, but that isn't an excuse, I should have messaged you," I apologize.

She blows out a breath. "Look, it's fine. Is that crazy bitch still outside?" she asks.

"I don't think so, but I do have something to tell you." I lower my voice as I look around to see if there is anyone around to hear what I am about to tell her.

"This doesn't sound like it's gonna be something I wanna hear." She tsks.

"Look, I am really thankful for everything you have done, but I have to leave." And of course it wouldn't be Frankie if she didn't let me finish what I was about to tell her.

"Leave, leave, where the fuck are you planning on going? You know you have some crazy fucking cunt following you right now, don't you?" she shouts.

"Yes, I do, and that is exactly why I am leaving, the reason she is following me around is because she feels like I am somehow a threat to their relationship...and we both know I am not." I sigh, wishing I was.

"Rosie, there isn't anything between them, she has problems, you know that. I was speaking with Nico and he said Gabe told him there isn't anything there. He has told her, but she won't have it." I hear something smash, and she starts to mutter her usual curse words, making me smile. I will really miss her.

"That doesn't make a difference, you know. The point is she thinks there is and as much as I wish there could be something between myself and Gabe, there can't be. I have so many things going on right now, and she is just the tip of the problems," I groan out loud.

"You know, Frankie, maybe in another life it would have worked, but not this one." I pause and think about how good it felt waking up with him every morning, just the two of us, and something I even wish we could go back to. In O'Connor's basement we had no one but each other. As sick as it sounds, it was there where our connection started. I look to the ceiling, well, it's where I knew he was it for me.

"We can work this out. You don't need to leave. You have the backing of us all, surely that is enough, and you know I can sort her out for you, right?" she tells me matter-of-factly.

"I do but that isn't it. I know she can be removed from this situation, but she isn't the only thing I have to worry about right now, and as much as it pains me to say this, they look good together. Maybe Gabe only thinks he wants me because I saved him," I tell her, voicing my fear. It's what I have thought for a long time but have never wanted to say out loud.

"Now you're talking crazy, but I can see nothing I say to you is going to change your mind." She sighs. "You will keep in touch, so I know that you're safe?" she asks.

"You know I will, but I can't let anyone know where I am going, not yet anyway," I tell her.

"I understand, but if you ever need anything, just say the word, we've got you." I hear the smile in her voice and know this is my chance.

"You mean anything?" I smile.

"Anything."

"Can you come by and feed Meow," I ask, nibbling on my lip, waiting to see what she says.

"You kept those fucking cats? I hate cats!" she shouts.

"They had nowhere to go and looked hungry," I tell her.

"Cats will eat anything, they'll be fine," she responds.

"You said anything." I smile.

"Fuck! Fine, I will get someone over there, but now you owe me for that shit!" She laughs. "Now, if you ever need something serious, I will be there."

"Fine, and thank you, Frankie." I disconnect the line before I get emotional.

I have to leave. I don't want Harridan waiting outside for too long. Pushing through the door, I look up and down the road but see nothing. I don't see *her*. I scrunch my face up in confusion, why is she not here? She has never let me down before. What if something happened to her? I start to think about all the things that could have happened, then I hear a can rattle down the alley and a meow. There she is. I turn on my heel and go to check on her one last time as my phone pings. Phew, Harridan.

Harridan: Shank is on to me

"Shit," I mumble.

Harridan: The Romano's have been asking why we met.

Double shit

Harridan: I am going to head out later, wait inside until I come for you.

I was worried she may not be able to come at all, but how in the hell did he know I had met with H? Shaking my head, I plan to ask her about it later. I will go and check on Meow before heading back inside to wait for Harridan. This is just a bump in the road. I start to call Meow as I head into the alley, then feel pain radiate through my head and the coldness of the concrete on my hands.

"He belongs to me, bitch, and I am going to make sure you remember that." I look up and that's when I see her... Fuck, Sophia.

CHAPTER 10

Gabe

I DECIDE TO LEAVE O'Connor for a while after being with him for a few hours just circling and cleaning tools in silence. You could smell the fear, which was my goal. Now all I need to do is maintain it until I decide to end it. Because I will end it.

Walking through the big double oak doors of Nico's house I hear Nico and Frankie talking in the kitchen, and she sounds pissed, so I decide to hang around outside and listen.

"She's leaving and says it isn't because of that mad bitch, but I bet it is," she shouts.

"She said it wasn't, so you have to believe what she told you, Frankie. She's a smart girl and knows what she is doing," he says, trying to calm her down.

"Don't do that, don't try to belittle what is going on here. I know Rosie knows what she is doing, and maybe there's more to this, but if that mad cunt wasn't part of this, she would stay, and we would work through whatever else is happening," she challenges.

What the fuck, Rosie is leaving? Where the fuck is she going?

"Evening," I say, entering the kitchen, and they both look at me and then back to each other. I know they are both thinking the same thing... How much did I hear? "So, anything you want to tell me?" I ask, raising my brow as I look between them both.

"Look, I don't know what you already heard," Nico tells me as he walks toward the counter and stands next to me, placing his hand on my shoulder, squeezing it reassuringly. "But I am sure there is more to this than we think, so we need to think carefully before we go all guns blazing." He taps my shoulder and heads back over to Frankie as I watch his mouth drop open slightly.

"You are fucking kidding me, right?" she shouts at him. "You were in the same conversation as me when I told you what she said to me about having to leave and it wasn't all about that fucking fruitcake Sophia." She raises her arms in frustration.

I see the way he looks at her and watch his jaw work overtime. He is trying to remain calm, to make sure I don't fly off the handle, but thankfully, I have Frankie here who is going to tell me what I want to know.

"So, where is she going?" I look over at Frankie because she is the only one I am going to get answers from.

"I don't know. She can't tell me until she gets to where she is going, apparently." She sighs as she leans on the counter, palms underneath her chin.

"And why not?" I push.

"Look, I told her you and Sophia were nothing, less than nothing, but I am not sure she believed it. She said even if Sophia wasn't a problem, she is only the tip of what she has going on right now." She stands, looking to the ceiling, and I know she is just as pissed off about this as I am.

"Do you have any idea why she met up with someone from the Soul Reapers?" I ask.

"No, I don't. It could be something from her past." She shrugs. "You know more than I do I would imagine, but maybe she knew them growing up, she was in a children's home." She runs a hand over her face, closing her eyes.

I can see how this is impacting Frankie, she really took to Rosie, they were close...well, as close as Frankie gets to people without fucking them.

"I am gonna head over, she may have left something behind, a clue of what's actually going on," I say turning to head out of the door. "And you." I point to Nico. "You need to arrange a meeting with Shank. We need to know what is going on, for sure. I know he knows they met up and we need to chat, but does he know she has now gone? What if she is in their compound?" I smile to myself as I shake my head at Nico. "They may be solid, but like you said, they look after family first. Whoever that bitch is, she's one of them, so he will be protecting her from us. Let me know when the meeting is set up." I exit through the big oak doors at the front of the house and slide back into my sleek matt black Audi R8 and speed off, wheel spinning, causing gravel to hit the underside of the car.

She has to have left a clue. She can't just vanish. Our story hasn't even started.

I screech to a stop outside of Frankie's apartment and see the light is still on, which means she is still here...she hasn't left yet. I could persuade her to stay. Getting out of my car and slamming the door closed, I walk toward the entrance and hear voices in the alleyway. It's probably just drunks but something feels off, so I head toward the sound and hear a voice I recognize.

"He belongs to me, bitch, and I am going to make sure you remember that!"

Fuck, that's Sophia. I peer around the wall and see Rosie on the floor with her hand to the side of her head. Sophia has hold of Rosie's hair, and her usual put together self is all disheveled and demonic looking.

"You two are together, so why are you even here?" Rosie asks between gritted teeth.

Sophia cackles. "Why? You know why. He still thinks he is in love with you, all because you saved his life." She drops Rosie to the floor and kicks her in the stomach. I look around for the best angle to tackle this as I can see Rosie struggle for breath. That's when I see the streetlights reflect off the gun Sophia pulls from the back of her jeans.

"Get up," she hisses and pulls Rosie to her feet. "I want to look you in the eyes when I put this bullet in you, then I can watch you take your last breath."

"Pulling that trigger will be the last thing you do," Rosie calmly tells Sophia, the cold expression on her face shows no fear like I would expect, but pure hatred. "You're right, I want Gabe, but you both made your choice, and you chose each other," Rosie sneers back.

"You know, when you're dead he will forget about you, and I won't regret a thing," she shouts as they both struggle for the weapon.

I have to do something. Moving forward, I shout, "Stop!" The click of my revolver is loud in the now silent alleyway, and both women turn to look at me. I have my gun pointing directly at Sophia. "Drop the gun, Sophia,"

I order, my heart thundering inside me. I have to shoot her before she kills Rosie.

She smiles at me, and I watch as tears spill from her eyes. “I love you, Gabe, and if I can’t have you, baby, neither can she.” Two gun shots ring out.

Mine and hers.

Chapter 11

Rosie

I FEEL THE COOL barrel of her gun press against my stomach, but I am not going to beg for my life, not from her. She already has the man I want, what else does she want from me? I don't even know why we are in this situation; she already has him! I work my jaw as my heart beats in my ears. Am I scared? Hell yes! Am I gonna show this bitch? Hell no!

"Pulling that trigger, will be the last thing you do?" I look her in the eye, feeling nothing but hate for the bitch in front of me. "You're right, I want Gabe, but you both made your choice, and you chose each other," I sneer as she digs the gun deeper into my stomach.

"You know, when you're dead he will forget about you, and I won't regret a thing," she shouts.

I grab for the gun and try to pull it from her grasp, struggling with each other, pulling the gun backward and forward.

"Stop!"

Sophia and I stand in silence and face the man behind the voice I know all too well. Gabe. Why is he here? The click from a revolver echoes loud in the now silent alleyway. His gun is pointing directly at Sophia.

"Drop the gun, Sophia," he orders.

I swallow loudly as I glance sideways to gauge her reaction. Tears pool in her eyes. She genuinely didn't think he would do this to her, believing they were in love and I was the one in the way. I mean, I didn't think that he would raise a gun to someone for me. I suck in my bottom lip as I watch the two of them stand off. I don't want to say anything to catch her off guard, as he may be able to talk her down.

She smiles at him, tears spilling from her eyes. "I love you, Gabe, and if I can't have you, baby, neither can she." Gun shots echo in the alley, and the pain is almost instant as we both fall to the floor.

The dead weight of her body lands on top of mine, and I can't breathe. I vaguely hear his voice calling my name, then a blurry figure comes to stand beside me, warm fingers rest on my neck.

"Shit, fuck!" I see him standing and moving around as he heads down to the sidewalk and out of my view.

Four legs take his place and lift me from the floor, carrying me to some kind of vehicle. I feel the bumps of the road, but I can't work out what's happening or if I am actually dead and dreaming all of this.

"La Madrina, we have you, you're safe now. We have the doctor on standby back at the house. We are almost there, please stay with us."

I hear them, but each time I go to respond, nothing comes out. My mouth is dry, and all I can taste is blood. One thing is certain, I recognize those voices. Massimo and Enzo. If I am here with them, what happened to Sophia? Oh shit, what about Gabe? What have they done to him?

I try so hard to speak but only manage to mumble, "Sophia..."

"Don't worry," Massimo assures me. "We tried to get you both, but Gabe Romano was on the sidewalk, so we didn't have time as he was heading back in when we got away in the car. We will locate her. We are just sorry we didn't get to you on time."

"Follow..." I try to breathe but the pain sears through my stomach. "Me?"

"We have been watching you, to ensure you come back to us." He nods. "We will track her down. She will no doubt be in the local ER, so she won't be too hard to find." He rubs my arm, trying to reassure me.

"Gabe..." My eyes drift closed, but I feel him shake me.

"Stay awake, La Madrina." He taps the side of my face gently. "We watched Gabe enter the alleyway and shoot the woman you call Sophia, it looks like he was trying to get you help, and that's when we came in to bring you home." He looks down at me and smiles. "You will be okay, we have everything the hospital does, so you will be in good hands. Everyone is waiting for you."

I don't know what happened, but I must have passed out from the loss of blood. I wake in a room that feels familiar in a really shitty way. It is like rewinding my life by a few years, a past I have been trying to run from, yet here I am once again attached to drips and in a makeshift hospital room come bedroom, with a doctor who takes cash with no questions asked.

"How do you feel?" He looks down at me, holding a clipboard in his hand. I mean, what the hell is he going to do with that, it's not like he can actually keep my records anywhere.

"Like I have been shot." I smile sarcastically at him.

He clears his throat awkwardly. "Right, of course. Well, you'll be pleased to know it was a surface wound, and we kept you under for a couple of days to allow time for you to heal."

"A surface wound, are you kidding me? I took a bullet in my body and you're calling that a surface wound?" I yell at him.

"So, what I mean is that it didn't hit any major arteries or organs, it was straight in and out." He starts to shuffle on his feet. "You did lose a lot of blood, so we needed to give you a transfusion, but overall, it was surface level."

"Massimo!" I shout. "Massimo," I call again when he doesn't come in straight away.

"What's wrong?" he asks as he comes rushing through the white bedroom door.

"Who is this?" I ask, nodding toward the doctor.

"The doctor, La Madrina." He looks at me with a frown, and I can see the concern across his face as he eyes the doctor, waiting for reassurance from him, but I don't give him the chance.

"Really? And how long has he been part of the *familia*?" I raise my eyes in question.

"Many many years, he is a loyal man, and he knows what he is doing. He is a surgeon at the local hospital." He smiles and places his hands together in front of him.

"Get rid of him, he is of no use to us going forward find a new one." I look at the doctor and see his Adam's apple move up and down.

"Ros-" Massimo goes to speak, and I raise my brow. "Sorry, I mean La Madrina."

"You're not questioning my choices already, are you, Massimo?" I smile sweetly at him.

"Consider it done." He raises his hand, and two men come in and take the doctor out the room. His screams can be heard down the hallway, getting quieter and quieter as they get closer to the basement.

Looking out of my old bedroom window, I know now is the time for me to shine. If Theo Conti thought putting me in this position would break me, he has it all wrong... This is going to be the making of me.

CHAPTER 12

Gabe

I GROWL AT THE constant ringing of Nico's phone. It feels like it has been ringing forever before he finally picks up.

"He-"

"I need you here at Frankie's old apartment with a van to transport Rosie, she's been shot," I rush out.

"What the fuck! One sec, you're on speaker, Frankie is here." He tells her what I said, and I hear a glass smash against something.

"Is she alive?" Frankie asks, her tone quiet.

"I don't know, she was when I left to call you, there was no fucking signal." I turn and head to the top of the alleyway, looking toward Sophia and Rosie, only Rosie isn't there. What the fuck!

"If that cunt killed her, I will make her pay," Frankie spits out.

"What the actual fuck, she's gone!" I tell them. "Get here now!" I hang up as I head to Sophia and see if she is okay. I didn't shoot to kill, just enough to knock her off her feet.

"Sophia!" I shout as I drop to my knees next to her. "Sophia, where is Rosie?" I shake her shoulders, trying to get her attention.

Great, so this is how it's gonna go, she's only going to respond with grunts. I guess I can work with that. I lift her up, and her arms snake around my neck, face buried into my chest. "I knew you'd save me, Gabe. You love me." Her voice is low, but I fucking heard her.

"I shot you, you remember that right?" I tilt my head away as she starts to run her fingers into the back of my hair.

She starts to laugh, but it obviously hurts somewhere as she stops abruptly. "Oh, I know that was an accident. You were just worried that scum bag would hurt me."

This woman is relentless, and there really is no way to reason with her... Well, there is one I can think of, and as if she can read my mind, Frankie and Nico pull up alongside the sidewalk. Before I know it, Frankie jumps out and opens the back doors of the dark blue truck, then she strides over to me and pulls Sophia from me.

"Oh, look what's just been dragged in." She smiles at Sophia, who tries to grip on to my shirt. "I think not, buttercup, you get to take a ride with me." She tugs her, and Sophia drops to the floor. Frankie bends down and grips her hair, pulling her to the back of the truck. Sophia screams as blood from the wound drips from her arm. If she thinks any of us here are going to help her, then she really has lost all sense of reality.

"Are you not going to tie her up?" Nico calls back to Frankie.

“Seriously, are you telling me how to do my job now?” Her hand lands on her hip, and she flicks her hair back staring him down.

“It’s better to be safe,” is all he says as he heads over to the driver’s side, getting back in and closing the door.

“You’re right. Let’s be safe.” Leaning forward, she grabs a clump of Sophia’s hair and smashes her face into the wooden base of the truck and blood instantly gushes from her nose, but she doesn’t make a sound.

“What the fuck, Frankie?” Nico shouts.

“It’s better to be safe.” She grins sarcastically and slams the back of the truck closed, walking toward me. “Follow us. We will get her to the yard and then work out what the fuck happened to Rosie.”

I head back to my car and jump in, following them both back to the yard. All the time my mind wondering what the fuck has just happened. How the fuck did she just get up and walk away from that? Where is she?

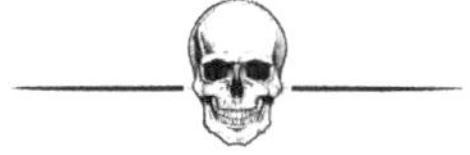

It doesn’t take us long before we are lining up at the gates. Nico must have called ahead as Tommy is already there, gates open, waving us in. Anger hits me as soon as my car goes through. I wasn’t expecting to be back so soon. I wanted to leave O’Connor to sit alone with his thoughts of what I could do to him for a while longer, but all because of fucking Sophia we are back here.

Two people have caused Rosie pain, and for what? What has she done to deserve any of this? She isn’t even a part of this world but keeps getting dragged deeper and deeper into it. Maybe she would be better off if I just left her alone. She is a sweet girl with the whole world at her feet, if she's even still alive. I slam my hands against the leather of the steering wheel. "Fuck!" Who the hell am I kidding. When I get hold of her, I am not letting her go again, no matter how hard she tries to fight.

"Are you coming, asshole?" Frankie shouts. "We don't have all fucking day." She swings open the truck doors and drags out Sophia, who appears to be coming around from the bang to her head earlier.

Slamming the car door, I head over but Tommy stops me. "He is still in there, barely alive. What do you want to do with him?"

"You have other spare containers for us to use?" I ask.

"Yeah, of course, but they don't have anything in them. This is the only one I have that is well equipped." He smiles. The sick bastard lives for this.

"That's fine, I can't see her being an issue. We will use the other one for her, and as for him." I nod toward the rusty blue container. "Feed and water him. I want you to build his strength back up, give him regular exercise when he is up for it." I smile and walk off toward Frankie.

"Hey," Tommy calls.

"Yeah." I tilt my head.

"Welcome back," he says as he walks away laughing, and I can't help but smile at his words. I do feel at home here. I was born into this life, but after everything that happened, I kinda lost my way, but now...now I am thirsty for blood and willing to do whatever it takes to protect those I love...family. She is family and I will find her, if not today, then I will turn the world upside down until I do.

"Frankie, head over to the container to the left, the other is still occupied," I inform her and point in the direction of the new one in front of the dock.

"Sure, does it have what we need inside? It looks like it's just arrived." She looks at it like it's something she's stepped in.

"It has and no, it hasn't. What do you think we will need?" I raise a brow at her. "Look at her. I think we can handle her, don't you?"

"Whatever. Let's just get her in there, we don't have all day to waste time sitting here chatting." She huffs.

CHAPTER 13

Rosie

THIS IS IT, THE time is now. I pull my phone from the bedside table and fire off a text.

Rosie: I am all good and back in NJ.

Harridan: Fuck, I have been calling. WTF happened?

Rosie: Long story, but I'm here now, so like you said, it's my time. Catch up soon.

Harridan: I got ya, bitch. Txt if you need anything.

I don't respond because that's how we are. We will always be there for each other, and I may need her connections. I have a plan, but I am not sure how it'll go, so I need to make sure I have everyone on side.

"Massimo," I call, and he enters quickly.

"Yes." His head bows, waiting for me to tell him what I need, but I am enjoying this moment as he starts to feel uncomfortable in the silence.

Smiling, I decide to put him out of his misery. "Call a meeting. I want the capos here in the next hour, no excuses." I lift my hand and dismiss him, and to my surprise that shit actually works.

Well, fuck me...

I get out of bed and move gingerly across the room to see what I have to wear. I need to look good for this meeting, they need to see I mean business, even if inside I am still a little unsure if it will work.

The next hour flies by, and I am standing in Theo's old office waiting for the men to arrive. Massimo and Enzo are already here while Rocco and Luca are on their way. Massimo is my new right-hand man until we discuss what the plans are moving forward, which is part of what this meeting will be about. Enzo runs the docks, well, he used to. I am not sure what they all do, so now is the time for me to find out. I hear voices as they approach the doorway, and Massimo moves forward to greet them. They all enter and stand in front of the desk, then looking at me, they bow their heads in unison.

"La Madrina, it's good to have you here," Luca says.

"Yes, we will serve you just as we did your father," Rocca assures me.

"You may all take a seat." I gesture toward the Chesterfields that have been placed in a semi-circle in front of my desk. "As you know, this was not something I expected, nor something I wanted, but I will be honoring my father's wishes." Calling him father makes my skin crawl, but I know that's what they expect. "However, I have a plan that will make us greater than we have ever been." I look around at them all and see I have their interest.

"The Romanos," I say simply.

They all let out a chuckle, and quickly clear their throats, realizing the lack of respect they're showing.

I narrow my eyes at them all as I continue. "Oh, you think they're untouchable? But if we can join the two families together, then we would be unstoppable," I tell them as I look each one in the eye. "What do you know about them?" I ask.

Enzo speaks first. "Look, I know that since Nico took over, they've been switching some of their businesses legit, not all of course, they have some financial company in the city."

"Okay, that's good. We used to have legit businesses, right?" I question.

"Yes, plenty, coffee shops, bakeries," he tells me.

"Perfect, what else?" I know about the club and the gym but nothing substantial as they never spoke business around me, which I was never bothered about until this very moment.

"They run drugs mainly, and they have a hold over the docks. We still hold the small area down the lower East Side, which is where Luca gets the deliveries, but other than that, they have it all." He shakes his head, and I can see that pisses him off.

"Okay, so basically, the Romanos have the monopoly?" I start to tap my finger on the desk, as I know the yard they have is also in New Jersey, but it doesn't cross into our territory.

Massimo stands and places his hands in his pockets and looks at me. "What *is* your plan?"

"A contract marriage." I smile, looking at their faces is priceless. They have no idea what I am on about right now, and to be honest, it is all a little crazy, but I am kinda flying by the seat of my pants.

"With who? Nico is with that crazy bitch, everyone has heard about her, plus there isn't anyone in the family to offer?" he tells me.

"Not Nico." I smile. "Gabe, and I will be the one he marries."

"What, you can't do that," he tells me.

"Can't I?" I smirk. "Set up the meeting with Nico Romano." I move around the table and stand directly in front of them all. "And make it so it's here." I raise my brow as I cross my arms.

"Whatever you say. I will get it done." He nods.

"For now, I want you all to carry on as normal, keep business running like before," I instruct. "In the meantime, I will look over the paperwork at what we have legitimately and work on that. And, Massimo, I want you to go through all the unscrupulous dealings with me." I smile at him.

"The rest of you, thank you for coming. I will let you know when I have everything set up. I want you to know your support means a lot to me." I gesture for them to leave, and as if on cue, they all stand, bow, and head out of the room silently.

I place my palms flat on the desk and blow out a sigh. There is only one way I am going to be able to do this. I wanted this to be me, just me, but with Gabe, I know I would be so much stronger. He gave me courage when I was at my lowest, and to be honest, I don't think I truly want to do this without him.

CHAPTER 14

Gabe

IT'S BEEN TWO DAYS, two fucking days, and she has said nothing about that night. All we've had are the pitiful sobs about how much she loves me and how I am better off without Rosie.

"I am sick of this. We haven't been able to trace her, and this cunt is no help!" Frankie shouts and she walks out slamming the container door behind her.

None of us have left here since that night. We're tired and tempers are starting to show. Frankie's is the first to snap. I don't know where she has gone, but hopefully when she gets back, she will have cooled down as we need answers. Sophia doesn't respond well to being shouted at, we worked that out early on. We assumed time would wear her down, but that doesn't seem to be working. She is playing us all for fools.

I hear grumbling outside and open the door to see Frankie pulling a surgical trolley along the dirt path, all sorts of items bouncing and clattering on top of it.

"What the fuck are you doing?" I ask as I bend and help her inside with it.

"Oh this, well, I have had enough. Two days is two days too fucking many." She turns and grabs a hose pipe, threading it through the gap at the side of the container, then grabbing the pole on the door, slamming the daylight out.

"So, Sophia, you don't want to tell us anything about where Rosie went... Are you sure about that?" she asks as she turns her over to her back and straddles her.

I see the small smile appear in the corners of Sophia's face, thinking she is winning, but the evil glint in Frankie's eyes right now tells me she will be in for a very rude awakening.

"Honey, you have just made a big fucking mistake." She shuffles forward so her knees have her head in a vice-like grip and then she switches on the hosepipe.

I stand back, leaning on the wall, and watch as Sophia starts to turn her head away, but Frankie grips harder, making it impossible for her to move. She tries to call my name between gasping and choking, the water constant, and her crying is smothered by the stream of water flowing freely over her face.

"Anything you'd like to tell us yet?" Frankie asks, moving the water away from her face, giving her an opportunity to speak.

"P-p-please, the doctor said I need rest," she splutters.

Well, fuck me! I look over to Nico, who is leaning on his hunches and watching Frankie carefully, he isn't paying attention to anyone else in the room, gaze transfixed.

"Wrong answer," is all Frankie tells her before she leans forward and pinches her nose and returns to spraying water on her face.

I watch closely, waiting to see if she is trying to speak, but nothing. Over and over she asks the same question, but all we get are tears and the same response as the last two days of how much she loves me. In a fit of rage, Frankie tosses the hosepipe away and looks over at me with a sinister smile.

"You love him?" is all she says to Sophia as she stands up and walks over to me.

She moves closer to me and whispers, "This will only hurt a little." She moves back slowly, giving me a wink.

Sophia still hasn't answered her, but I think she must be in shock, I know I am. Frankie has done a complete one-eighty in the space of five seconds.

"How much?" she asks as she walks to the trolley, picking up a small pocketknife. Flicking the blade up, she tests the end with the tip of her finger, pulling it back quickly when it draws blood. "Ooh, that's sharp." She chuckles.

"W-what's happening?" Sophia looks around at all of us.

"It's okay, you won't tell us what happened to Rosie, we know that. We have been here for two days," Frankie tells her and looks over at Nico and me. "If it were up to me, we would have fucking killed her in the first two hours, but apparently, these two grew a fucking conscience. Anyhoo, that doesn't matter now, that's all in the past, because, no matter what we do, you're not gonna give us what we need, right?" She smiles sweetly at her.

"N-no, it's not–" she starts but Frankie cuts her off.

"Tell him you love him one last time?" she tells Sophia as I feel Frankie walk beside me, running her hand up my arm.

"I thought..." Sophia says as her mouth drops open when she sees the same as I do, the reflection of the blade at the side of my temple. "No, no..." she shouts. "Please don't!"

I feel it before I have time to move. Fuck she's good! On instinct, my hand reaches up to cover my neck where Frankie has nicked me, but apparently, that isn't all she wanted. I feel her knee take me out from behind, and I fall to my knees.

"Wait, please..." Sophia shouts as she tries to sit up, tears streaming down her face "I-I don't really know much, all I know is two men came in and took her away."

"And?" Frankie pushes.

"Erm...they, they called her something odd." She closes her eyes, as if trying to recall.

"What, what did they call her?" Frankie yells.

"I can't think," she splutters, spit spilling from her lips as she looks around frantically, hoping someone will stop this.

Nico is not gonna help, he is totally fixated with the woman who is holding a knife to my fucking neck, and he is enjoying it more than he should be. The sick fucker.

"You better try fucking harder because his time is running out, sweetheart." She taps the knife to my temple and cackles.

"It was La something... wait, La Madrina, yeah that's it." She sighs. "Please, let him go."

Fuck! La Madrina.

Frankie leaves my side and strides over to Sophia and kneels behind her, taking a clump of her hair, pulling her head back. "There, that wasn't so fucking hard was it." She kisses her cheek. "Sleep tight, you mad cunt." She slices the knife across Sophia's throat. She lets her head drop with a thud to the floor and stands up and watches as she chokes on the blood spilling from her mouth. Frankie doesn't move until she has watched the life leave Sophia's body.

"What the fuck does this mean?" She turns to look at us both, and if you hadn't just witnessed what she'd done, you wouldn't have been able to tell. "What the fuck is La Madrina?" She raises her arms.

For the first time since we have been here, Nico's eyes move from Frankie and land on me. "The Godmother," he replies, his tone serious.

Frankie is laughing so hard she is bent over, holding her stomach. "Fuck off! Rosie, The Godmother? a.k.a. the fairy godmother, that bitch couldn't hurt a fly."

I slam my fist on the side of the container. "Stop! What the fuck is happening here, what have we missed? She's been with us for months, so surely if she was part of another *familia* we would have known?"

"Get the men together and meet at the club," he tells me as he strides past, gesturing his head for Frankie to follow him and despite the frown on her face she follows.

Chapter 15

Gabe

The four of us are sitting in Nico's office in the club when we hear the door burst open, and Frankie stands there with her arms folded.

"So, you think that you can have this meeting without me, huh?" she sasses.

Tommy, Tony, Marco, and I all look between her and Nico waiting for his response, but he says nothing, just nods for her to enter.

The constant beeping of Marco's phone is starting to piss me off. "Will you switch that off," I tell him. "That fucking beeping is getting on my fucking nerves, man. I can't think straight."

"Yeah, well, when you have incompetent staff, they always have something they need you for, you know, not being able to think for themselves." He rolls his eyes and stares at Nico, as if trying to prove a point.

Marco has been running the legitimate side of our businesses and in charge of NIC or National Investment Corp. I smile when I think how arrogant Nico is, all the businesses have his name in there somewhere.

"Enough of that, we have more important things to discuss, and I can't remember how many times I have told you she isn't incompetent, you just need to fuck her out of your system and move the fuck on." Nico stands and heads toward the drink cabinet in the corner of his office, pouring only himself a drink.

We update the others on what's been going on, and they all look confused, no one suspected Rosie of being a part of another family.

"Look, there was never a time where we discussed any part of our business while she was around, legit or otherwise," Tony says. "I have been at the house pretty much the whole time, and she seemed like any other woman, naïve. Hell, I assumed she thought we were just businessmen."

"We are, kinda," Tommy says with a smile.

"Fuck!" Marco stands with his phone in his hand. "You're not gonna believe this." He looks around the room at us all.

"Don't just fucking stare at it, share with the rest of the room," Nico demands.

"It's a request, a meeting–" he starts and then Nico's phone pings.

He looks down, his face lights from the screen of his cell phone, only glancing up, not really needing to say anything as we know he has also had a request.

"So..." I urge.

"The Contis, they want a meeting on their territory tomorrow at noon. They have a proposal," Nico relays the information.

"Marco?" I look over at him.

"I had the same, it says they want to discuss some investments." He frowns.

"Something isn't right, we should all go." I stand and head over to the bar and get myself a drink, Nico, as usual, is being a shit host.

"We have to go alone," Marco says.

"Shit, do you think this has something to do with Rosie?" I swallow the clear liquid in one gulp.

"Only one way to find out," Nico tells me. "We will go and see what this is about. The Contis are small-time. Theo died a couple of years ago, and his men started a war to avenge his death, but things have quietened down recently. The other *familia* around the States were requesting a meeting, but they kept declining. I guess now is the time to find out why?"

"Is that it? You're just gonna wait until tomorrow?" Frankie asks. "This can't be Rosie, her surname was Carmicheal, not fucking Conti?"

"It means nothing, and yes, that's it. I won't be questioned on this." He eyes her, waiting for her to dare argue with him, but there must be something in his eyes because she purses her lips and doesn't say another word.

Nico's phone pings again, and we all look over as he reads.

"Shank is happy to talk," is all he says.

"Right, when?" I ask.

"Tomorrow, meet me back here and we can call him," he lets me know as he looks over at Frankie and lifts his head. "Now, I am sure you all have other things to be doing. I will call if we need anything further." He starts to leave and looks to Marco. "Be here in the morning."

"Wait." Tommy stands and looks at us all. "Look, I didn't know Rosie very well, and I'm sorry, Frankie, I know you're worried, but the Contis? All we know is Theo died, and they went quite after the war they declared over the Blancos to avenge Theo's death."

"Right." I look at him. "What's your point?"

"Everyone assumed Theo killed his wife, but we all know what this life is like, it's hard, and not one that you want to show any weakness in or show anyone something or someone that means the world to you, you know what I mean, your Achilles heel. Once people know that...you're fucked." He glances at Frankie.

"What are you getting at, Tommy?" She huffs, knowing what he is saying but refuses to believe anyone would be able to get to her, which we all know is wrong. I am sure she has worked out that Nico has security on her 24/7 and acts like she doesn't know.

"La Madrina could be her, and she has finally decided now is the time to show the world who she is and is playing her hand." He leans against the desk, folding his arms across his chest.

"Say that's true, where does Rosie fit into all this?" I question.

"Hey, I don't know, I am just thinking out loud here. From what you're all saying, Rosie doesn't fit into our world, she was too naïve to have lived in it, and that makes more sense. She could be an outstanding debt that needs collecting," he states, shrugging, and honestly, it makes sense, but if that's all true, then she could be in a lot more fucking danger this way. And I don't want to wait until tomorrow to find out.

"If that's the case, then they obviously want something from us." Nico frowns. "They won't do anything to her until they have negotiated with us. They know they won't get anything from us if she's dead or injured, if anything, they will fix her up from the shooting and use that to get more from us." He nods as if that's going to reassure me, and I can see Frankie doesn't look too happy about it either, but she stays quiet.

"The plans stay the same. Meet me here in the morning, and we will speak to Shank before I leave with Marco." He turns and leaves, Frankie following on his heels.

We follow them out while Tony, Nico, and Frankie stay at the club, which surprises no one. I follow Marco who is looking at his phone.

CHAPTER 16

Rosie

I NEED THIS TO go well. I have to play this carefully, really think this through. I needed to get Nico here alone and the only way he would consider that was to have at least one of his men with him. The only way that would work is by bringing Marco, and that wouldn't be a bad thing considering I want to discuss switching some of our businesses legit... Well, not me but Massimo. If I show my face now, then this wouldn't go the way I wanted for the right reasons.

Today, I am going to have to speak through him, they can't see me. If they do, this won't be taken seriously, and they will automatically think they have the upper hand. I think if we were joined, then we could be a force. I just need to get Nico on board with that, and I don't want him to just do it because he knows it's me. We will be equals, I have to believe that, which is why I have to do it this way first.

"Massimo," I call, and as usual he enters. If only everyone I know obeyed me in this way. At first, I found it odd, but I have gotten used to it. I know if I had Gabe at my side then I could do great things. I just need to make sure Sophia isn't going to be a problem.

"They will be here in an hour or so. We have everything set up and the cameras will show if they come alone," he assures me.

"They can't see me today, so you will take this meeting. I had the paperwork written up, but we need to persuade Nico a contract marriage is the best way to go," I tell him.

"I have gone through the businesses and there are some he will find beneficial, maybe we can use those as leverage. The port we have is undetected and means the usual routes can be used for legitimate business. It will get its usual checks but will always come back with nothing. The NYPD will soon get fed up when they never locate anything from the crossings." I smile at him. "I know they have officers in their pocket, but they can't always get them out of shit, but we can assist in that." I purse my lips as I think.

"Good move. I think that will be a sweetener." He nods and smiles at me.

"We have a lot to offer them, we just need to sell it, and once the families join, we will be a force to be reckoned with." I stand from my desk and head toward the kitchen. "Oh, and make sure they are aware I am okay. They will want to see evidence, so bring them to the garden after the meeting, and I will be sitting on the terrace. I will be over at the rose garden."

"Yes, La Madrina." He bows his head and leaves.

I watch the maids in the kitchen preparing for our visitors. I have them preparing Nico's favorites, knowing that sometimes the best way to a man's heart is his stomach. I mean, I want everything to go smoothly. Will this work, probably not, but it's worth giving anything a go.

Grabbing a coffee mug, I move around them placing my cup under some fancy barista style coffee machine, pressing a button and hoping for the best. When I left here, I tried to forget everything about this place. I knew how fancy it was, but I had never been around it all. But this kitchen is a chef's dream, all high-end silver finished appliances, an island that takes way too many steps to get all the way around, and silver counter tops like you get in restaurant kitchens. Honestly, I would have preferred to cook for myself, but I would take forever to actually find where anything is in here.

Leaving them too it, I walk back through the swing door to the white tiled hallway, which is now void of any pictures. I asked the men to remove them all because seeing them was too hard, and they seemed to buy it. In all honesty, looking at Theo's face turned my stomach. I want to remove every part of him from this place, and I will do it bit by bit.

The rooms upstairs are all being redecorated, including his bedroom, and the lounge room has been gutted. All that is there now is a bare floor and white walls, ready for me to decide what I want to do with it. That is something I will decide with Gabe...not that he knows it yet, but we will live here together. I have set my heart on it and gutting every room in this place will mean we can both start from scratch. We deserve this, and I have to believe we can build something and leave Sophia in the past.

"La Madrina," I hear Massimo call as I start to open the patio doors. "They're arriving and came alone," he tells me before I have to ask.

"Perfect. You know what to do," I tell him as I turn my back on him and leave, heading over to the rose garden, which gives me a view of the office. Only from here, they cannot see me.

I take a seat on the soft floral blanket that has been placed there ready for me and inhale deeply, looking at the clear blue sky. Moment of truth, now's the time to see if what I want to happen actually comes to fruition. I have been banking on this. I haven't got a plan B.

CHAPTER 17

Gabe

THE DOOR TO NICO's office is ajar. Pushing it open, I roll the stiffness from my neck. It's been a long night and drifting off in the chair in Tony's gym hasn't done my neck any good. I wasn't expecting to see anyone here. Nico is never in before noon. That was one of the unspoken rules: I run the early hours, and he gets to walk in whenever the fuck he pleases.

But today, he is already here.

"Fuck me!" I mutter, pausing on the threshold. My brother sits behind the massive mahogany desk, suit jacket draped over the chair, and shirt sleeves rolled up. A single glass of whiskey rests by his hand...untouched. "Didn't think you knew what sunrise looked like."

Nico's dark eyes lift, holding my gaze.

I smirk, knowing I must have touched a nerve. "Lemme guess, you spent all night at the club and kept

Frankie tied up just so she wouldn't interrupt our meeting, huh?"

The silence that follows is heavy. He didn't move, didn't blink. He just let the words hang there like smoke.

When he finally speaks, his voice is low. "Watch your tongue, *fratello*."

I realize I may have gone too far and lose the smirk, lifting my hands in mock surrender. "Relax. It was just a joke."

"This isn't the place for jokes."

"Yeah." I cross the room, dropping into one of the leather chairs opposite the desk. I lean forward, placing my elbows on my knees. "You're right. My mistake. I guess I am nervous about today, *fratello*," I explain. I can't get Rosie out of my mind. What if she is hurt? What if they have done something to her? I move those thoughts to the back of my mind for now and look at my brother. "Let's get back to business."

Nico nods in agreement. "Good."

Dragging a hand through my already messy hair, my bravado now gone. "Shank. You think we can get to him early?"

"I already reached out." Nico taps the untouched glass. "He's free all morning, said we should call whenever we're ready."

"Perfect." I gesture to the phone. "Let's not waste time then."

Nico presses a button, putting the call on speaker. The ring buzzes through the office, loud against the stillness of the morning. On the third chime, a gravelly, rough voice answers.

"Yeah?"

"Shank," Nico says evenly. "It's Nico Romano. I've got my brother Gabe here with me. You're on speaker."

There is a pause, then the sound of a cigarette being drawn on. Shank's voice comes again, deeper now, commanding. "Then listen closely, I don't like repeating myself. You're asking about Rosie," he went on. "H said she knew her from a past life, you could say. She was helping her with something, no business of yours. That's all there is to it. The night in question, Rosie asked her for a ride, said she needed to get away from some crazy bitch that's been stalking her."

Gabe's eyes narrow, shifting forward in his chair, wanting more. "That's it? You expect us to believe—"

Shank cuts him off with a growl. "You can believe whatever the fuck you want, Romano. Rosie's not my concern. She wanted out of a bad situation, H gave her wheels. End of story." His words echo in the quiet office.

Another drag of his smoke, then Shank's tone hardens. "We've always respected each other's boundaries. That's how it stayed peaceful between your family and my club. I suggest we keep it that way."

Nico's hand stills on the desk, his voice calm and clear. "I feel the same, Shank. We appreciate your time."

The line clicks dead.

The office is suddenly too quiet; the only sound is the faint ticking of the wall clock.

I stand, shoving the chair backward, running both hands over my face. "Fuck, he's stonewalling us. We got nothing except some bullshit about a stalker." I sigh. "He knows we know all about Sophia, and she already spoke to us about that."

Nico finally lifts his glass, still not taking a sip. He stares at the amber liquid as if it might hold the answers. "It's not nothing. It tells us Rosie's playing in deeper waters than she wants us to know."

“Deeper waters?” I laugh out loud. “He practically told us to fuck off. You heard that warning…‘respect the boundaries.’” shaking my head, I look at Nico waiting for his response.

“That’s why we don’t push him,” is all he says.

“Don’t push him?” I pace the room. “We need answers, not some biker’s bedtime story.”

Nico finally drinks, slow and measured, the way he does everything. He sets the glass down with care, then looks up at me. “And we’ll get them. But not from Shank.”

I stop my pacing, hands clenched at my sides. I can feel the fire burning inside me. “Then where?” I spit.

“The Contis,” Nico says simply. “That’s the only place answers will come from now.”

Marco interrupts when he enters. “Morning, I trust you are both ready for the call with Shank?” He sets his takeout coffee cup on Nico’s desk, which earns him a scowl from Nico. I can’t help but smile, after everything we’ve spoken about this morning the one thing that pisses him off is the fact Marco placed his travel cup on his desk without using the coaster.

“Coasters, Marco…use them,” Nico states.

Marco follows orders and places the cup on a coaster, and you can see the tension in Nico’s shoulders ease…unbelievable.

“We already had the call, nothing to report. I was just telling Gabe the only place we will get answers from now is the Contis.”

“Well, it’s a good job we have a meeting set up with them today.” He looks at both of us with a smile.

CHAPTER 18

Nico

WE ENTER THE OFFICE of the Conti familia, and it feels off. I've been here before, but the decor has been changed, it is definitely more feminine. La Madrina has certainly made her mark.

It's too soft for the kind of men seated inside it right now. Roses perfume the air, like this wasn't their office but whoever it was had just been here and left their presence lingering behind... I have smelled this perfume before, but I can't put my finger on where, or more specifically who it belongs to. I lean forward, my voice clipped. "Before we talk, I want proof. If Rosie's dead, there's no deal to be made."

Massimo smirks and nods once. A guard crosses the room and pulls open the French doors. Sunlight spills in, unveiling the garden beyond, roses in every shade of red and white. And there, seated beneath an iron arch on a picnic blanket is Rosie.

Her sundress is crisp and white. She gazes at the roses in a way that feels unnatural. She doesn't look caged. She doesn't even look watched. She looks as if she belongs here.

Marco exhales, satisfied. Proof. She is alive. I let my eyes linger. There is something about her, the way she sits, the certainty in the tilt of her chin. I can't fucking say what has me on edge, but the sight of her unsettles me.

Rosie looks too composed for a pawn.

The doors shut, cutting off the garden, and the men turn back to the table.

"And what of Sophia?" Massimo asks, his tone probing. "She was meant to be Gabe's bride. Will she be a problem?"

"No. She's not a problem. She's dead. And Gabe never loved her." I keep my voice low.

He learns forward, steepling his fingers. "Then the path is clear. Gabe will take the marriage. The ports will open. Rosie is free."

Marco's jaw tightens. "You make it sound simple. But Gabe-"

"Doesn't have to love her," Massimo cuts in smoothly. "He doesn't even have to want her. He only has to understand what this union brings. Rosie is just the price."

I look over at Marco and see he is unhappy with this. He stands to express how he feels, but I shake my head slightly, letting him know now is not the time, and he follows my instructions.

Persuading Gabe to marry someone who isn't Rosie won't be easy, but Gabe will be made to see this is the only way we can set Rosie free from La Madrina.

The real question isn't whether he will accept the bride, it is whether the bride will accept a man whose heart belongs to someone else.

CHAPTER 19

Gabe

I NEED TO LET off steam, and the best way to do that is at the yard. O'Connor has been waiting long enough. Entering the container the stench is strong, iron and urine linger in the air.

"O'Connor, how have you been?" I ask as I swing the doors shut with a slam.

He doesn't answer, but if looks could kill, he would have the upper hand. The men have done a good job piecing him back together. His face is healing nicely, his clothes are cleaner, and his cheeks have filled out.

I wanted to watch him die slowly, but I have neither the time nor patience. I should have left him the way he was but something inside me wanted to have the man from before standing in front of me when I have him take his last breath.

I always preferred to play with people's minds...the things you can get people to do is amazing.

"Just kill me," he spits out. "That's what's going to happen, so why are you keeping me here?" he asks, and I can see the slight tremble in his bottom lip, which makes me smirk.

I go to answer him when the doors open and light pours in from the sun beaming outside. The door shuts with a hollow thud behind Nico, his presence pulling the air tighter.

"I figured you'd be here," Nico states cooly as he strides in, keeping his eyes fixed on me.

I head over to the cabinets, turning my back on Nico, shoulders stiff beneath the weight of everything unsaid. The tip of the knife digs a hole in the countertop as I wait on what he has to say.

"You saw her?" I say without turning. Keeping my voice low.

Nico paces in silence, then walks a circle around O'Connor.

"Fuck, tell me," I command.

"She's alive," Nico says finally. I know I should be relieved, but there is something in his voice that doesn't make it sound like it's a good thing.

I turn, my eyes burning into Nico. "Alive? That's all you're gonna fucking give me?"

I watch Nico as he works his jaw. He seems off as he walks over to the cabinet, grabbing two glasses and pouring us both a whiskey. He passes me one before he takes a swig of his. "She looked...well. Too well. Not like someone begging for her life. Like someone waiting for the rest of us to catch up to her."

My hand tightens around the glass until it cracks, whiskey bleeding down my knuckles like amber blood. "Then what the fuck do they want?"

Nico's eyes darken. He speaks like a priest delivering a final rite. "They want you to marry a ghost."

My laugh is hollow. "A ghost. You're telling me I can't have her, but I can sign my life to a stranger?"

"Yes, a stranger," Nico says, his voice steady. "A contract marriage. Whatever person La Madrina chooses. No face, no identity until the vows are spoken. You marry, Rosie lives. You refuse, she disappears."

I hear chuckling from behind, and I see red. O'Connor sees the situation I am in and that I have to sacrifice...again. A red mist blurs my vision as I pull the pistol from the back of my slacks and with one shot to his head, he slumps forward...dead.

Seeing him like that angers me more, he got off lightly. I let my anger take over, but he is the least of my worries.

I stalk toward Nico, my voice cutting through the air fiercely, unshaken. "Then I'll do it." I slam my bloody hand down on the counter. "I don't give a fuck who I have to marry. I'll put the ring on her finger...whatever it takes." I place both my hands on the countertop and lower my head. A low growl leaves me, and my voice drops low. "And when Rosie is free, I'll burn every single one of them for thinking they could play with me."

Nico holds my stare, something grim flickering in his eyes. He'd gotten what he came for. But in the pit of my gut, I sense unease. The doubts still linger, I can tell, but I can't risk anything. I know he says that Rosie didn't look like a prisoner and that she looked like something else entirely.

We know what I have to do, and whatever I have to do now, Rosie will always be mine, one way or another.

CHAPTER 20

Rosie

I AM SITTING UNDER the archway that overlooks the gardens. Vines curl against pale walls, and the fountain murmurs, steady and peacefully.

"La Madrina," Massimo calls out, breaking the silence.

"Over here." I grab his attention as I watch him come toward me. I close the accounts I had been pretending to read and tilt my head upward. "You have spoken with Nico,"

Massimo's jaw flexes. "I have."

"Tell me," I ask, my voice calm, although my stomach is coiled with tension.

He takes a seat across from me. "Nico has not rejected the marriage contract outright. He acknowledges that what we've proposed is...beneficial. To your house and to his. The business opportunities, the alliance...it is all clear to him."

I keep my expression blank, though relief rushes through my body. "But..." I prompt.

Massimo exhales slowly. "He asked for proof, just as you expected. Proof that you are not being kept here against your will."

I narrow my eyes. What could be wrong with that? If they see me, then why would there be a problem? "And you showed him."

"I did. I let him see you here, in your garden." Massimo's brow furrows, remembering. "And it unsettled him. His face changed. He looked at you as though you were playing a role too well. As though he couldn't decide whether you were actually a prisoner."

I tilt my lips faintly, though my hands stay folded on my lap. "Nico doubts. That is his nature. Frankie and he are more alike than either like to admit. But doubt won't stop a contract from going ahead."

Massimo leans forward. "He didn't mention stopping it. But he does seem hesitant. And Gabe..." Hearing his name makes me still. Massimo continues, like he hasn't seen my reaction to him mentioning Gabe. "Nico said that convincing Gabe will be difficult. That Gabe wants you. Enough to make the union complicated."

The words fall like stones into still water, sending ripples through my chest.

I swallow once carefully, not wanting to sound eager. "He said that outright?"

"He did. And more." Massimo's tone drops lower. "Sophia is dead. To bind Gabe to you would be, as he put it 'marrying him to a ghost.' He admitted it will not be easy. But he also made it plain...if he decides it will be done, then it will happen. His word is final."

The silence stretches between us, filled only by the fountain's endless trickle. I look away, my gaze settling on the roses climbing the wall.

"Gabe," I whisper.

Massimo's eyes narrow, wary. "Does this surprise you, La Madrina?"

"Yes." My voice is soft. "I hadn't known. I thought he was in love with someone else. I thought he saw me as...well, just the woman that saved him and nothing more. But desire...desire changes everything."

Massimo shifts uneasily. "Desire also makes men reckless. If Gabe believes he should have you—"

"Then he has me, and we will be a force," I cut in, my tone sharp. "Do you not see, Massimo? If he wants me, then our families will be unstoppable."

"You could have just told him who you were," Massimo says carefully.

I turn my gaze back to him, my smile slow and deliberate. "Where would the fun in that be?"

"You're risking a lot."

"I risk what I must," I say simply. "Nico would have always doubted La Madrina, but he would have always underestimated me as Rosie. When all is revealed, he will understand my reasons."

Massimo stares at me for a long moment, then bows his head. "Very well, La Madrina. It is not my place to question you."

My smile lingers as I sit back, composed once more. "It is enough that you carry their words to me. Leave the rest in my hands."

Massimo rises. "As you wish."

I watch as he leaves, waiting for him to disappear around the corner before blowing out a deep breath. My hands are trembling in my lap, not with fear, but with the thrill of all that's been revealed.

Gabe wants me.

The knowledge twists through me like heat, unsettling and intoxicating. I had never intended to be desired. Of course, it was what I had hoped for, but the contract was strategy and alliance. But now? Now it's more. My heart beats faster, not from dread but from satisfaction.

The roses sway in the courtyard breeze, petals catching sunlight. I watch them with a hint of sadness, knowing why all these roses where planted in this garden and who was responsible. Her, my mother, which is why I haven't had them all dug up, but it hurts my heart to know that she was once here, submitting to the monster that walked the halls of the mansion.

Maybe I could be that monster, the one that kills all her demons. I have more power than I ever dreamed of, and now I have issued the contract, I know every fire begins with a spark.

Maybe, I can be the flame.

CHAPTER 21

Nico

THE GLOW FROM MY phone is the only light in my office, reflecting off the oak desk and the gold trim of the liquor shelves behind me. The club throbs outside, bass-heavy music vibrating through the walls, muffled laughter, the clink of glasses.

My office is silent in comparison, just the ticking of the clock on the wall reminding me time isn't on my side. What if I'm wrong? What if Rosie is a prisoner and this deal really will release her?

Although Gabe is happy to go through this for Rosie's sake, is this a trap?

I decide to play the long game and see what Conti's plan is. The deal, albeit unusual, is a good one for us, it will open new opportunities for us. I type out a message carefully.

Nico: The deal is on. Gabe will marry whoever La Madrina chooses. But Rosie walks free first.

My thumb lingers over the screen before I send it, the muscles in my jaw tightening, hating the fact he has been put in this position. If this was a straightforward business opportunity, things could be different.

The reply comes quickly.

Massimo: You ask for a lot, Romano.

I read the text again, and my lips twist into something between a smile and a snarl and type back, my fingers hitting the keys harder than necessary.

Nico: I don't ask. I demand.

The phone stays silent. The bass from the club pounds harder, rattling in my chest like a second heartbeat. I push away from the desk, pacing to the bar in the corner and pouring more than usual in my crystal glass and knocking it back in one gulp.

Rosie. Was she locked away in some basement, treated like a pawn? Or worse, was Massimo lying, keeping her as leverage, a prisoner in velvet chains? The thought twists like barbed wire inside my chest. My phone buzzes, taking me from my thoughts.

Massimo: You'll have her. At the wedding. That is the exchange.

I slam my fist against the desk, the sound echoing through the office. At the wedding. Of course. He wants an audience. Grinding my teeth, I type back.

Nico: You play dangerous games.

The pause stretches long, then comes the answer, deliberate, smug almost.

Massimo: You will not be sorry. The Romano's alone are a force. But the Romano's with the Contis...that is something different. Something untouchable.

Sinking back into my chair, the leather creaking beneath me. My father's voice whispers in memory—*never trust a Conti.* But times have changed. Once, the Contis ruled New Jersey like kings. Then they vanished, leaving only rumors of betrayal and exile. Now they have returned.

Curiosity gets the better of me as I pick up my phone and respond.

Nico: You went silent for years. Why now?

Massimo's reply comes after a long pause.

Massimo: Because we have her back. La Madrina. With her, everything is back on track.

That name cuts through me like ice water. La Madrina. The ghost queen of the Contis. Whispers about her had fed the underworld for the last few years. After the assassination of Theo, there were talks of betrayal and other assassination attempts within, but then they went to war with the Blancos, who they believed were the ones to kill their Don and kidnap his heir...La Madrina.

Without her, the family had crumbled. With her back...

With the pounding of the music outside, I pinch the bridge of my nose. If La Madrina truly had returned, this wasn't just a marriage. It was the resurrection of an empire. And Rosie, sweet, sweet Rosie, was standing in the middle of it, a bargaining chip passed between monsters. My phone lights up and vibrates again.

Gabe: When's the exchange?

My throat tightens as I type quickly.

Nico: She'll be freed at the wedding.

The reply is instant.

Gabe: You trust them?

I stare at his words; he should know the answer to that.

Nico: I don't trust anyone outside this family.

Silence. No reply.

Gripping my phone tighter, fucked off at the lack of response from Gabe, I go to throw it across the room when it buzzes in my hand.

Fuck...Massimo again.

Massimo: See you soon, Romano.

Leaning back, I steeple my fingers below my chin and nose as doubt creeps in. I really don't like this guy, something seems off, but I just can't put my fucking finger on it. All we have to say that Rosie is safe is Massimo's word, and in our world, words are as dangerous as bullets.

The wedding is coming, and with it, the truth.

Either Rosie walks free or Massimo proves he's been keeping her as his prisoner all along.

And if that is the case, then no alliance, no promise, no family name will save the Contis from the fury of the Romanos.

CHAPTER 22

Gabe

ONE WEEK LATER

The storm has been clawing at the city since dawn, rain lashing against the sidewalk. Lightning split the clouds and thunder banging like a drum. A shitty day to go with the shitty mood I am in.

No guests. No flowers. No music. There appears to be only one man waiting outside the church...Massimo.

He stands beneath the awning, smoke curling from the cigarette between his fingers, coat collar turned up against the storm.

Nico's car pulls up first, the black Mercedes gliding through sheets of rain like a predator. He steps out, suited in black with a face carved from ice. His presence enough to silence the very thunder. I followed in a black SUV, my shoulders tense.

I hate this. Every part of it.

Massimo drops his cigarette, crushing it beneath polished shoes, and greets us with a smile that doesn't reach his eyes. "Gentlemen," he says, "you came. Good. I was beginning to think you might test La Madrina's patience."

Nico doesn't flinch. "We said we'd be here." His tone dangerous.

Massimo's gaze flicks to Gabe. "Then you know the terms. When the contract is signed, when the vows are sealed, Rosie is free."

The name feels like a blade in my chest. Rosie. My Rosie. My only reason for agreeing to this farce of a marriage.

"And until then?" I ask, my voice rough and bitter.

Massimo smirks. "Until then, she waits."

The storm rattles the stained-glass windows of the church. I can feel my fury boiling over, too sharp to contain. I turn, my fist flying, driving it through one of the colored panes. Glass shatters, raining down like jewels, cutting deep into my knuckles. Blood streaks my skin, warm against the cold rain.

Nico grabs my wrist, squeezing hard enough to make me wince. "Control yourself," he orders in a low growl. "Bleed later. Not now."

With a low chuckle Massimo looks over at me. "This way, gentlemen"

The doors groan open, and the three of us step inside. The church is dim, lit only by candles that flicker against stone pillars. At the altar, there she stands, my bride-to-be.

A woman dressed in black. Her veil is heavy lace, draped low over her face, and her gown clings to her, showing every curve. Even from a distance, I catch the glint of crimson beneath the hem, red-bottomed heels, sharp as blades, heels carved into the shape of a dagger.

The air in my lungs stills. What the fuck is this? Who dresses like a widow to their own wedding?

I should have refused. I should have torn this church apart brick by brick. But the weight of Rosie's freedom presses against my chest like a gun barrel. With my jaw clenched tight enough to crack, I step forward. My shoes echo against the stone floor, each step dragging me closer to a fate I despise.

The woman doesn't move, doesn't bow her head, or acknowledge me. Only the faintest tilt of her chin when I reach her side. What the fuck?

I lean closer, my voice a low growl meant only for her. "You're not her. Where the fuck is Rosie?"

Silence.

The priest clears his throat and begins the ceremony, his words solemn, echoing through the vaulted ceiling. I barely hear him. My gaze locked on the woman, trying to pierce the veil, trying to find anything, eyes, lips, something familiar.

But she is still like a statue.

The priest turns to her. "Do you take this man as your husband?"

For a heartbeat, she doesn't move. Then, slowly, she nods. A small dip of her head, nothing more.

No words. No vows.

"She's mute," Massimo says smoothly from the pews, his smirk cocky. "But she understands her duty."

I inhale deeply, curling my hands into fists. I want to rip the veil away, to demand answers, to burn the entire church down if it means getting to Rosie.

The priest turns to me. "And do you take this woman..."

"I don't," I spit out, loud enough to silence the candles themselves. I glare at Nico, then Massimo. "This is bull-shit. I want Rosie."

"Finish it," Nico hisses under his breath, eyes sharp as knives.

"Say the words," Massimo echoes, voice almost mocking. "Or your sweet Rosie stays in chains."

My bloodied hand trembles at my side. I try to catch my breath. The woman shifts then, turning just slightly, and a faint trace of her perfume drifts across the air.

It hits me like a shot of whiskey. Familiar. Intoxicating.

Rosie.

The scent pulls memories to the surface, her laughter in my ear, her skin beneath my hands, the way she used to bury her face in my neck when she'd snuggle up to me when we were recovering.

Was it possible? Could it be?

I stared at her through the veil, heart pounding so violently it drowns out the storm.

No. La Madrina wouldn't dare. She wouldn't risk...

But the scent doesn't lie. My body knows it's her, even if my mind is screaming otherwise. It is her. It has to be.

My throat tightens, and I lower my voice to a hoarse whisper. "Rosie?"

The woman's chin lifts just slightly, the barest fraction, but enough.

Hope and horror slam into me all at once.

If it is her, why hide her? Why force this masquerade? Unless...unless this was La Madrina's cruelest play of all. To give me what I wanted but twist it into something poisoned. My stomach knots, rage curling with desperate need. I want to rip the fucking veil away, to grab Rosie and run.

Massimo's gaze is on me, wearing a smile he isn't even trying to hide, and Nico's warning grip presses into my shoulder.

The priest's voice cuts back in, patient but stern. "Do you take this woman to be your wife?"

The church goes silent, except for the rain tapping at the windows.

I clenched my jaw, blood dripping from my cut hand onto the stone floor. I stare at her, at the shape of her beneath the veil, at the faint hint of a smile hidden in the lace. It is her. I can feel it...but why is she smiling?

And if it is, then saying no means condemning her to La Madrina forever.

I force air into my lungs, the words ripping from my throat. "I do."

The church doors slam against the storm. And when the priest pronounces us husband and wife, I lean in, trembling with fury, need, and disbelief, my lips close to the veil.

"If it's you, Rosie," I whisper so only she could hear, "I swear I'll find a way to burn this whole world down to get us out."

The woman says nothing. Only the faintest tremor runs through her shoulders.

And I know.

It is her.

Chapter 23

Rosie

He knows, my body gave me away. His presence alone makes me feel things I cannot explain, it's like the 4th of July going off inside my chest whenever he is near me. I glance sideways, and I know he wants to say something, but I must speak out now. They have to know I orchestrated this marriage for a reason.

Inhaling deeply, I lift the dark lace veil from my face and turn to face Gabe, looking deep into his ocean blue eyes and refusing to drop contact even though I can see the confusion written across his face.

"I believe you have to finish the service," I say unwavering, waiting for the priest to pick up where he left off.

He clears his throat and continues, "Gabe you may now kiss your bride."

It takes a moment to sink in that it's me! I'm his bride.

Without hesitation he steps forward and leans in, kissing me briefly and pulling me closer, whispering in my ear, "Rosie, I will save you from this, I promise." He squeezes my hand to reassure me.

He doesn't understand. I don't think any of them understand that I didn't speak up to get this over with because I wanted out of here, I spoke up because I wanted them to see me...see me for who I really am. It looks like it's going to take more than that to show them who I really am.

We sign the papers, and I am ushered outside the church quickly.

"I think you leave too quickly," Massimo calls. "La Madrina wants to see you back at the house...all of you." He looks over at Nico and then back to Gabe, his smirk makes my skin crawl.

I've put up with him for far too long, but he's been useful to me and has done everything I've asked, without question or hesitation. However, I believe his time will soon be up.

I hear a low growl leave Gabe as he pulls me close to him, as if he is protecting me from...well, me, but he doesn't know it yet.

"You said she would be free once the papers were signed." Nico's voice is icy, matching his glare.

"Oh, she will be. There's just one final thing La Madrina wants to do before this is finished." He grins as he heads off into the shadows, wrapping his leather coat around him, protecting him from the pouring rain.

"Mother fucker," Gabe grumbles. "We should never have trusted those fuckers."

"The deal may be done, but the ink is yet to dry, my brother," Nico says calmly. "If she doesn't follow the terms, then neither will we."

I watch closely as he pulls his phone from his pocket, dialing a number. I don't know who it belongs to but hear the order loud and clear.

"Get your soldiers to the Contis and prepare them for war." He ends the call and nods at Gabe as they separate, getting into their vehicles.

My heart starts to beat so fast like a thousand drummers bursting to get out. I am so close. I have to hold it together. The door closes behind me as I sink into the soft black leather of Gabe's SUV, waiting for him to get into the driver's seat. I am not surprised he doesn't have a driver, he likes to do things for himself.

His door slams shut, echoing around us, and he leans over, his hand reaching for my cheek. "I will keep you safe from now on, angel," he tells me as his lips press hard against mine. He pulls away quickly, leaving me wanting more.

The engine roars to life as he speeds away, following Nico and leading the way to my estate. I am not sure they will like what I have in store or even expect it, but what I have done is done for the right reasons. Neither of them would have taken me seriously at the start, and had I not done this, I would never have known Gabe's true feelings for me...or believed them. This was the right thing to do for me, and I stand by that. I know if one person understands, it'll be Frankie. I hope she comes with them tonight.

Turning, I watch as he concentrates on the road, his hand gripping the wheel tightly, working his jaw so much I think he may even break a molar.

I clear my throat. "Do you think Frankie will come?" I hear the hope in my voice.

"Do you want her there?" His brow raises as he turns to look at me briefly.

"I do," is all I say as I turn and watch the streetlights go past quickly.

"Then she'll be there." He taps on the phone which is connected to the dashboard.

I see the response flash up with Nico's name at the top

Nico: I couldn't stop her.

"She is meeting us there," is all he says, and we make the rest of the journey in silence.

I want to ask him why he didn't tell me how he felt, why he just carried on as if we were friends, but I guess when you think back the same could be said for me. Why didn't I say something, why did I just wait around for him.

Looking at my reflection in the window, I screw my face up. I don't have time for shoulda, woulda, coulda now. Too much has happened, and I have to keep moving forward.

We pull up to the iron gates and the soldiers on watch let us through. Massimo didn't waste any time in getting home. He has Enzo next to him, which could make the next part of the plan tricky. But the Rosie of yesterday isn't the same as I am today. And they will soon see what I am really made of.

Chapter 24

Gabe

Fuck only knows what is going on. I have been watching Rosie out of the corner of my eye since we've been alone, and I think Nico is right...something is off. I can't put my finger on what exactly, but I would have expected her to have been more relieved to see us.

The Conti Estate sits on the outskirts of New Jersey, and the scent of rain lingers in the air. We drive in behind Nico, keeping our eyes on Massimo and some other guy by his side. Thankfully, I hear cars filing in behind us, the gravel kicking up with the speed they are entering the estate. They're here. We're not alone.

Entering the mansion, candles flicker against the polished marble and dark shadows lurk in every corner. Rosie leads the way like a queen leads her court. She heads through to the main office, and I glance across to Nico and watch his jaw tick. He is pissed.

We've been double crossed, but how and why?

Nico strides in front of me, which fucks me off because he knows I should lead. He could be walking into danger. But his dark, cold eyes tell me he is on a mission, and I know no matter what is happening right now, no fucker is going to put him down. He is a crazy mother fucker, and I know he is thinking what I am. And that alone means he won't need any of us here to help him.

I turn when I hear the others come through the front entrance, and as usual Frankie is charged with energy. The smile on her face tells me she is just as crazy as my brother. She thrives in moments like this, just the thought she may get to kill someone tonight makes her as happy as a pig in shit.

Tony, Tommy, and Marco all file in, and they don't look as happy. My gut twists at the thought she would betray any of us. If she has, I won't let any of them pull the trigger. We all stand in front of the big oak desk with Massimo behind it and Rosie closing the door behind us. Her heels tap against the floor like a ticking clock. The wait is killing me.

She takes Massimo's place, and he nods. He and Enzo stand to her other side, both bowing.

What. The. Fuck!

I catch her eye, and I see determination there. No matter what she has to say now, something deep inside is telling me I have to protect her, from what I haven't worked out, but I know I would kill for her. These men I am surrounded by are my family, but if it came to choosing, I don't even need to think. I know how I feel and the woman in front of me is mine. I won't give her up for anyone... No matter what she has done.

She smiles softly at each of us. "Now everyone is here...we can begin."

"What the fuck is this, Rosie?" Nico frowns.

Frankie starts to bounce on her feet and clap. “Oh, this is fucking exciting!”

“Enough.” Nico glares at Frankie, and she rolls her eyes in response.

“First, before I go on, I have some general housekeeping that needs to be done,” Rosie starts as she leans forward and reaches for the drawer in her desk, pulling a pistol out. The metallic click of her gun echoes in the stillness. In one fluid motion, she turns and two shots ring out.

Massimo drops first. Then Enzo, their bodies motionless under the flickering light.

I watch as the others all react and pull out their weapons, yet she doesn’t flinch...This isn’t the Rosie I know...or knew.

“They served their purpose,” she says quietly, her voice steady. It surprises me how unaffected she is by what’s just happened. “Now, please,” She gestures lightly with the gun. “Sit.”

Silence fills the room, and we all look at each other, shocked at what just happened, well, all except for Frankie.

“Fuck yeah! I knew you had it in you, Rose.” The smile is that of a mad woman, but they share a nod. They get on so well, and it appears their bond is only strengthening.

Of course Frankie would understand. She thrives in the madness, in the shimmer between beauty and brutality.

One by one, we all take a seat opposite her, chairs scraping across the floor. The Rosie I knew wasn’t like this, she was soft and gentle, and from what I knew had never even handled a gun... Fuck, I didn’t even know she knew about our world. It appears Frankie knew a different side to her, but she never mentioned any of this.

I continue to watch her, waiting to see a crack in the armor she is wearing but nothing, and it only makes me fall harder. I feel the love burning from the inside. She has endured so much and is standing in front of us holding her own without anybody by her side.

She straightens her black wedding dress. The lace clings to her like a second skin, and it is almost like the darkness of the dress is seeping into her soul. We are all waiting for her to speak, and when she finally breaks the silence, we are all listening.

"For years, men like you have built kingdoms on the backs of women like me, breaking us down to make yourselves better. Daughters, wives. Lovers, promises made and broken in smoke-filled rooms." She huffs out a laugh, but a smile is the furthest thing reaching her face.

Stepping closer to us she comes round the desk. "I played your game, I followed your rules, smiled when I was told to, I obeyed...until I took matters into my own hands." This time the smile that reaches her lips is sinister. "When Teddy, my father, took my mother's life, he didn't know it but he had the chance to let me walk away, to leave me and let me live my life, but he chose otherwise." She laughs. "That was his first mistake. Then I learned rules were meant to be re-written."

Nico's voice cuts through the air. "You've lost your fucking mind."

Her head tilts and a small, dangerous smile touches her lips. "Maybe, or maybe I've found it."

Frankie leans forward, her chin resting on her hand, her eyes gleaming. "This is better than any wedding I've been too."

Rosie ignores her, her eyes catching mine, finally, and for a fleeting moment, I saw it, the armor in her expression cracked.

"You are tied to me, Gabe, and there is nothing you can do about that," is all she says before moving on, walking back behind her desk, not giving any time for us to respond. "The Contis," she says slowly, "have lived too long in the shadows of men. Teddy's second mistake was assuming he was going to live long enough to arrange my marriage but amending his will to tie me to this family for the rest of my life. I am La Madrina." She smiles and looks at Nico. "Our families are tied by marriage." Her eyes land on mine, and I can't help but feel pride in her.

CHAPTER 25

Rosie

THE SILENCE PRESSES AGAINST me like a weight I can't shake. The others have gone. Nico storming off in anger, Frankie giving me her seal of approval, which to be honest I expected, and now it is just me and Gabe. Just the two of us in the echoing space that felt alive only moments ago.

The smell of death fills the air, and I step over the bodies of the two men who helped me get to this point...I will deal with those later. I swallow, trying to steady my racing heart. I want to retreat. So much has happened, and I need to give myself some measure of control over the mixture of feelings that have been swirling around in me for days. And despite all that, part of me wanted to stay.

There is no real choice, I have to stay. We have to discuss what's going to happen from here.

"Let's go," he says, turning and walking out of the office and down the empty hallways.

I follow but I'm not sure he knows where he's headed. "Where are you going?" I ask, trying to keep my voice steady.

"Where's the master room? We need to talk but not in there and not right now." He gestures toward the office.

Walking past him I lead us to the bedroom, unsure of what I'm leading myself too, but he has a point. We do need to talk and most of the other rooms are now empty. Gutted, to remove every trace of Teddy, to start afresh with Gabe...only he doesn't know that yet.

I feel the cold breeze as I enter the room and turn to face him. He leans casually against the doorway of the master bedroom, arms crossed, his expression unreadable in the dim light. His presence always made me feel both nervous and safe. I no longer feel nervous, not in the way I was before. I was always worried I would never be good enough for him, that I needed to be perfect all the time...but not now.

I take a cautious step toward him. "You stayed," I say, my voice barely above a whisper.

He lifts one brow, the smallest trace of a smile tugging at the corner of his lips. "I said we could discuss things tomorrow," he replies "But...I stayed."

Something flutters in my chest, a strange mix of relief and anticipation. It was as if I'd been holding my breath and, finally, someone reminded me how to exhale. "I...I didn't expect you to," I admit, stepping a little closer, feeling the subtle shift in the air between us.

His eyes, dark and unreadable, catch mine, and I feel a strange heat crawl up my neck. "You shouldn't assume," he says softly, almost a murmur. "You've learned by now that assumptions can be dangerous."

I nod, biting the inside of my cheek. He is right. I have learned, painfully, that trusting my own instincts isn't always enough. And yet...there was him. Always him, standing there, a constant I'd always been able to depend on, but somehow, I'd allowed myself to forget that and all because of one woman...Sophia. I'd let her words overshadow his.

The room feels smaller now, the empty furniture and drifting curtains filling the space. I shift my weight, unsure whether to speak or stay silent, to bridge the distance or retreat into my self. But then, as if sensing my hesitation, Gabe steps forward, closing the gap between us.

"You've changed," he says, and it isn't a challenge, nor a casual observation. It is a statement layered with something I can't quite name. Respect, admiration, maybe even relief.

"I...I've had to," I reply. "I was left with no choice."

He studies me for a long moment, and I feel exposed under that steady gaze. It makes me uneasy but in the best way possible.

"I always knew you were a fighter," he says finally, his voice low and deliberate. "I thought you left all your fight in the basement, but I'm glad I was wrong."

Warmth spreads through my chest...he sees me. Truly sees me. And it isn't pity...it is recognition.

"I had to learn," I say quietly, my hands brushing together nervously. "I couldn't...I couldn't just let things happen to me anymore."

He nods, stepping closer. "And you did. That's...good." His voice has softened, a rare vulnerability threading through it. I can't remember the last time I heard it sound so unguarded.

For a heartbeat, the world falls away. Just the two of us. The empty room, the drifting curtains, the scent of the rain through the window. And then...he reaches out, his hand brushing against my cheek, thumb tracing along my bottom lip.

"You've got fire," he murmurs, leaning slightly closer. "But...don't mistake fire for recklessness."

My chest tightens. "I know," I whisper. "I just...I needed to know if you were...if you wanted this too. If you want me."

His eyes soften, dark pools of something I can't name but that make my knees feel weak. "You've always been mine, Rosie. In ways that matter...that no contract could define. But now...now it's different. I want this with you. All of it. Every piece of you."

I can't stop the small laugh that escapes me, a mixture of disbelief and relief. "So...you're saying you don't regret the marriage?" I ask, teasing lightly, though my heart pounds in my chest.

He smirks, that confident, infuriating smirk. "I never did. Not really. But what matters is what comes next. Not what we signed...what we choose now."

My throat tightens. All the doubts I'd held onto, all the fears about power, control, and whether he even wanted me...evaporate under the heat of his gaze. "Then...let's choose, together," I whisper.

Gabe's smile softens into something tender, almost vulnerable. "I'd like that," he says, his voice quiet. "But...you should know. I'm not letting go of you easily. Not ever."

I step closer, closing the last of the distance, feeling the weight of all the unspoken things between us, fear, longing, anger, love. And I reach up, resting my hand against his chest, feeling the steady beat of his heart beneath my fingers. “I wouldn’t want you to,” I say, my voice firm, though trembling slightly with emotion. “I don’t think I could, even if I wanted to.”

He leans down, his forehead resting against mine, a gentle weight that somehow grounds me in a way I hadn’t realized I needed. My heart swells, the years of fear and frustration melting into something warm and undeniable.

“Then we’ll do it together,” I say softly. “Step by step. Choice by choice.”

He presses a gentle kiss to my forehead, a promise wrapped in that quiet intimacy that makes my knees weak and my chest feel impossibly full. “Together,” he echoes.

I rest my head against his chest, listening to the steady rhythm of his heartbeat, and let myself finally breathe. The wind stirs the curtains, sending shadows dancing across the walls, and I feel...safe. Not from the world, not from the past, not from the chaos of everything outside this room, but safe back with him.

And that is enough.

The house is silent, yes, but in that silence, we found a new kind of noise, the quiet murmur of two hearts learning to trust each other, two people discovering that love, even after pain and mistakes, could be enough to carry them through anything.

“Tomorrow,” he murmurs against my hair, “we start anew. No contracts, no games. Just...us.”

I nod, smiling, feeling tears prick the corners of my eyes. “Just us,” I echo, letting myself savor the moment, the intimacy, the promise. “And...I think I like that.”

He presses one last kiss to my temple before stepping back slightly, just enough to look at me properly, his eyes dark with warmth and something dangerously tender.

"Good," he says. "Because I don't plan on letting you go anytime soon."

We found each other again. And that...is everything.

CHAPTER 26

Gabe

SHE THINKS THIS MOMENT is all about tenderness...she's wrong. It's about me claiming her as my own. She may be La Madrina to everyone else, but she will always be my angel. I know she needed clarity about what this was for us. She let Sophia get into her head, which meant she had to go through all this alone, but now there is nothing but us, and together we will be unstoppable.

My hand reaches for the tender column of her neck, and I grip gently at first, watching her eyes widen in surprise. Pushing her back, she crashes into the wall, taking her breath away, and the fire that was alight in her eyes earlier returns. She wants this as much as I do, and I have waited long enough to claim what will always be mine.

I keep one hand on the soft column of her neck while the other roams freely down her lace covered body, finding the slit in her dress, giving me access to her smooth legs. She's smart, and this is proven to me even more when I find the knife attached around the top half of her leg...protection. She may have felt like she needed it before but no longer. Sliding it from its sheaf I make use of the sharp object. Releasing her neck, I take hold of her dress and glide the blade down the front of the dress. Her breach catches, tongue peeking out to moisten her perfect plump lips.

I make quick work of removing the dress and discard it on the floor, leaving her standing in nothing but a black thong. Her breasts are full, nipples pebbled, aching to be sucked, her hips arching forward slightly, as if inviting me to make a move. I can smell her arousal. I know she is wet and ready for me; I can see the evidence on her panties. Tonight should be about savoring her, but seeing her in front of me, exactly how I want her...I am not going to be able to wait.

"Kneel," I order and without any hesitation, she kneels.

I unbuckle my belt and slide it off, tossing it across the room, it clatters as it hits the floor. I watch her jump at the unexpected noise. Losing my pants, I stand in front of her with nothing but my dress shirt. I grip her hair, pulling her head back to get a better look at her face. The shadows of the room cast a light across the top of her head, and she truly looks like a fucking angel.

I run my thumb across her bottom lip and smirk at her. "You know what to do, angel."

"Wha...but I..." she starts.

I laugh. "But nothing. In here, in these moments, you are angel...mine, mine to do what I want with." I lean down so we are eye to eye. "You will do as I command, always...and not just because I tell you to...but because you want to. You *will* beg me, I promise." I wink and stand up. "Out there, with everyone else, you're La Madrina, and you call the shots." I nod.

I watch her throat bob as she swallows, but she nods in agreement.

"Now, I won't ask again, you know what to do."

This time without hesitation, she leans forward and opens her mouth, but instead of taking me in fully, this angel turned demon chooses to work her tongue up and down my shaft.I groan, leaning one hand against the wall behind her and the other tightly in her chocolate locks, pulling her head backward.

"Now's not the time to tease..." I yank her head harder this time, and her mouth opens as she moans in pain. I thrust my thick, aching cock inside her opening, the warmth of her mouth feels like heaven, and her groan goes all the way to my core.

I move back and forth, fucking her face relentlessly. She can't keep up and saliva builds, dripping from her chin. This is quicker than I would have liked, but we have the rest of the night for me to worship her body.

Her hands move to my thighs as she starts to moan around my shaft, her head moving faster than my thrusts, and her hips move, trying to get friction where she needs it most. Looking down at where her deep brown eyes have blown to pools of darkness, she drops one hand and teases her clit once, twice and then explodes, her groans hitting every nerve inside me.

I follow her, my cum filling her pretty little mouth, and I watch as she tries to swallow fast enough to stop it from escaping and spilling down the side of her chin. She looks exquisite.

With my hand tangled in her hair, I pull her up, which only arouses her further. So my angel likes to play a little rough. I find her lips with mine and kiss her deeply. We start to fight with our tongues, but I win. This is my time and she will take every drop I give her and in every hole I desire.

Sucking her lip as I move away, her mouth follows mine. "You look so good on your knees for me, taking every bit of what I have to give you. This is only the beginning, and I am going to own every part of your body, just like I own your heart."

CHAPTER 27

Rosie

OH GOD, PART OF me thinks I am dreaming now everything I wanted is finally happening. When I arranged the contract for this marriage, I thought that when he found out it was me, he wouldn't be happy, but now we are both finally on the same page.

I look at the man in front of me, the man who is controlling me in the best possible way, who has ended life for me as I know it. And I couldn't be happier.

I still feel the warmth of his cum that filled my mouth, and his possessive kiss that no matter how hard I tried, I wasn't going to win.

"On the bed, face down, ass in the air." His voice is commanding, and I don't hate it. I don't hate it at all.

Standing on shaky legs, I go over and climb on to the bed. The dampness between my legs has my cheeks blushing, and I raise my arms to cover my tummy. No matter how many times I go to the gym, I never seem to get the flat stomach Frankie has, so I look everywhere but at him.

"Don't do that, never be ashamed of how you look or feel. You're beautiful and I want to see all of you." He strides over, taking my chin in his thumb and forefinger, turning my head to look at him. "And I do mean all of you." His smirk is sensual. "Now, on the bed, angel."

I follow his orders and feel the softness of the sheets on my knees as I move further up the bed. Turning to look at him, I watch as he uncovers his body, revealing the six-pack he hides beneath it.

"Face forward."

Swallowing nervously, I do as instructed. I feel the coolness of the blade touch my skin and flinch.

He chuckles. "Now's probably not the time to flinch, angel, you have to trust me. I know what your body wants...and needs."

Taking a deep breath, I steady myself and concentrate on the cold sensation against my warm skin, it's followed by the sound of fabric tearing and the cool breeze against my pussy as he frees me from my panties. His hands grip my thighs as he widens my legs, causing me to fall forward. He groans deeply, almost animalistic.

"Fuck, your pussy is dripping, and I haven't even touched you yet."

The thought of him just looking and not touching is killing me. I want his touch badly, I crave it.

"Please, I need to feel you." I know I sound needy, but I don't care. I have wanted this moment for so long, and he is making me wait.

"And you will...soon." I hear the amusement in his voice. "You know, for so long, I have stood alone, touching my aching cock, thinking about how you would look. How you would feel. How you would taste. And nothing, and I mean nothing, was ever close to the real thing." His voice is breathless, and I glance over my shoulder again as I see him just looking at me while his hand is gripping his thick shaft, his movements getting faster and his breathing getting ragged.

"Please," is all I say, begging for him, wanting anything from him right now, yet getting nothing.

"You like this, you like the thought of me getting off to you lying here naked. On display just for me. Your body gives you away." He leans forward, and I feel the dip in the bed where his weight presses. His warm breath softly caresses my thighs, and he sucks in and moans. I feel the lightest pull from my pussy when he moves back.

What the hell. "I thought..." I start to say.

"Oh, angel, I don't need to lick your pussy yet." His hand caresses my ass. "Your juices were trying to escape, and I could only watch it drip from you for so long... You taste better than I ever could have imagined."

The thought sends chills across my body and an ache to my core.

"I know what you want, but you're just gonna have to wait, angel."

"Wait," I say, my voice a whisper. I don't think I can wait any longer. I could pull the gun from my side table and force him to fuck me, but that wouldn't be right...would it?

"It'll be worth the wait, trust me." His hands snake up my thighs and start caressing my ass, and I let out a groan, each squeeze only heightens the pleasure I feel.

I freeze momentarily when I feel his fingers glide across my asshole. This is new to me, but right now I will take whatever he has to give. My body relaxes with his touch, and my hips move in sync with his strokes.

"Hmmm, you like that," he purrs.

I can't speak, all the saliva from my mouth has dried up and been replaced with cotton wool, and the more I attempt to wet my lips the worse it gets.

"Normally, you'd be well lubricated here, you have enough for me to use, but I am a greedy man, Rosie, and I am saving that for myself." His voice has grown dark with lust.

The warmth of something dripping in the crack of my ass, makes me jolt in surprise. I feel him start to caress the moisture around my hole. The wetness comes again and this time I hear it, the spitting sound from his lips. I should be disgusted but I am anything but.

His finger presses harder, entering me, and I drop my forehead on to the bed, his finger moving in and out as more moisture is added from his mouth. The movements from his finger become faster, and it feels uncomfortable at first, but the more he continues, the more I want.

He moves forward, his knees spreading my legs even wider, and I feel his body touch mine as he reaches his other hand forward. "Spit," he orders.

I don't question it and just spit onto his fingers. His body straightens, and his wet fingers replace the one already fucking my ass.

"Count with me." His finger is already inside. "One..." His voice sounds strained.

"One," I whisper.

"Two," he groans as I feel another digit sink into my ass. I hiss at the intrusion but the pain eases and is replaced with pleasure.

"T-two," I stutter, trying to control my breathing. I am close to coming but don't want this to end.

"Three..." I feel his warm breath as he exhales across my ass, sending chills along my spine.

"Ahhh...I think...I think I'm gonna come," I rush out.

"Tut, Tut, Tut," he says. "That's not what I told you to do, was it, angel?"

"S-sorry." I swallow loudly and take a deep breath. "Three..."

"Good," is all he says, his fingers continuing to work back and forth, my hips matching the rhythm, and I have no choice, I can't hold it anymore. I start coming and feel my ass squeezing his fingers buried deep inside me.

"Look at you, so fucking beautiful!" A deep groan leaves him. "You know, you look like you're gonna take my cock well, angel."

Chapter 28

Gabe

I HAVE NEVER SEEN anything as fucking stunning as the woman in front of me right now. I have imagined this over and over and yet nothing comes close. I squeeze the tip of my cock, trying to prevent myself from coming. The next time I come, I am going to be deep inside that pretty little pussy of hers.

I look down and watch it glistening with her juices, just waiting for me to devour them. I remove my fingers gently from her ass and admire her gaping hole, tracing the outline, just watching the aftershock of her orgasm. Her ring contracts, and my jaw mirrors it. It's no fucking good. I have always taken what I wanted, and right now, I am a hunter who has found his prey. Now I just need to go in for the kill, and there is going to be nothing sweeter.

My big palms cover her ass cheeks, and my lips greedily feast on her asshole. Her groans start off low and become untamed as I refuse to stop. Turning over, I lay flat on my back and pull her pussy flat to my face and urge her to ride me, but I sense her hesitation.

"Take your pleasure, angel," I growl, my head reaching upward, getting another taste.

"I-I don't want to suffocate you." Yet, despite her concerns she lets out a needy little cry when my tongue meets her pussy, encouraging her to sit.

"You won't. Take what you need from me, angel." My hands grip her luscious hips and seat her exactly where I want her. I feel her relax and start to move tentatively...until she starts to feel pleasure.

Her hand rests back on my chest, and she starts to ride my face, her juices coating my lips as I feast on her like she is my last fucking meal. A low, rough grunt escapes me, and my hand finds my cock, trying to give myself some relief.The only thing that will do that now is feeling the warmth of her pussy, but not until I have taken every last drop of her orgasm. I feel it as her legs start to shake and a desperate scream fills the room. Her wetness covers my face, and she attempts to move away.

"Stay," I order. Now I know what heaven tastes like, I'm sure as shit not gonna let her move away because she's become bashful.

Having my fill, I guide her limp body to the bed and watch as she lays there content in what we've just done.

This is just the beginning, the night is still young.

Her body is relaxed, goose pimples dance across her skin, and a small smile plays at the corners of her lips. I dip my head down and take her lips in mine, kissing softly, tasting each other, before I pull back and watch her eyes flutter open. For a moment I see the flicker of confusion. Ah, she's unsure what's happening.

My heart beats wildly in my chest, looking at the woman lying in front of me. She's a contradiction. She was so soft and caring back when we were held captive, and yet only tonight did she stand in front of me and kill two men without hesitation because they've served their purpose. But when we're here like this, looking into each other's eyes, it's like nothing has changed at all. Only that time and misunderstanding robbed us of being together.

"I love you, angel." My voice is low, but I know from the look in her eyes—eyes filled with tears she refuses to shed—she heard me. I don't wait for a response. I take her lips again, this time with more urgency.

Pulling her center closer to mine I line my aching cock up with her soaking entrance and thrust in without warning. She breaks the kiss, releasing a breathy moan, her warm breath caressing my cheek.

Our hips move faster and faster together, and the once silent room is now filled with the low moans of pleasure, and the sound of skin hitting skin.

"Oh, Gabe," she whimpers. "I'm gonna..."

"I know." I place my thumb on her chin so we are looking directly at each other. "Come."

Her pussy grips so fucking tight, making me roar out my own release, filling her with my warm seed. Pulling out, I watch as my cum drips out and smile because I know now that she is full of me.

"I love you too." Her voice is soft but certain. She reaches for me, and I lie next to her. She places her head on my chest, and I realize this is the first time in a fucking long time I feel at ease.

I just have to remember what we have in this room and when we are together is what is important, because outside these walls...well, that's something else.

CHAPTER 29

Rosie

THE SUN HAS FULLY risen, shining brightly across the bedroom floor. I stirred first, letting my eyes adjust to the light, still heavy with sleep. Gabe's arm is draped loosely around me, anchoring me, and the steady rise and fall of his chest beneath my cheek is almost hypnotic. Even in the quiet of morning, there was a presence that demanded attention without even raising a hand or a voice.

"Morning," he murmurs, voice rough from sleep but calm, commanding. His dark eyes finally meet mine, and I feel that pull, that silent power that has always made my heart race, even when I trusted him completely.

"Morning," I whisper back, smiling softly.

"You're thinking," he says, almost amused, though the corner of his mouth twitches into the faintest smile.

I laugh quietly, brushing my fingers across his chest. "Maybe. Or maybe I'm just glad you're here."

He leans closer, resting his forehead against mine. "I'll always be here," he says. "Even when the world tries to pull us apart, even when everything goes wrong. This...us...it stays."

I close my eyes against his touch, savoring the comfort. "It feels like it," I murmur. "Last night...I realized I don't have to fight everything alone anymore. Not when you're here."

"Good," he says, a low rumble beneath the words. "Because you never will. Not with me. Not ever."

There is something in the weight of his certainty, the calm authority that has always drawn me to him, that made me shiver...not from fear, but from longing and from the safety of finally letting myself surrender to the trust I built.

We lie in silence for a few more moments, listening to the soft stir of the house, the wind brushing the curtains, the distant hum of the city beginning to wake. Then Gabe shifts slightly, sitting up and stretching, though he keeps me close, his hand on my waist.

"Come on," he says. "We have the day ahead. We can't let it slip past us."

"I don't want to move," I admit, though a small smile plays on my lips. "I could stay like this forever."

"Not forever," he says, leaning over and brushing a light kiss over my temple. "But long enough for you to remember that you belong here. With me. And long enough to face the world knowing we have each other."

I feel the thrill of that weight, of that authority, and let it wash over me, not resisting. "I do belong here," I whisper. "With you."

"That's good," he murmurs. "Because I don't plan to let you go. And I want you to start today knowing exactly where you stand...with me, safe, and wanted."

I laugh softly, leaning up to press my lips to his briefly. "Then I'm ready," I say. "To face it all. With you."

His hand slides up to cup my cheek, tilting my head slightly, and I feel the intensity in his eyes...the same quiet command, the same pull, the same presence that left me under his spell the night before. "That's my angel," he says. "Strong, defiant, and finally knowing you're allowed to let go."

The words make me shiver again from the warmth of trust, the thrill of surrendering fully to someone who had earned it. "And you?" I ask softly. "Do you ever let go?"

He smiles faintly, leaning in close enough I feel the heat of him without even touching. "I let go," he says. "But only when I know it's safe. With you, it's safe. That's why I'm here."

I rest my forehead against his, closing my eyes, letting the truth of his words sink into me. "Then I trust you," I say simply. "Completely."

"Good," he murmurs.

I laugh softly, letting the sound mix with the early light filtering through the curtains. "Then we're aligned," I say, matching the calm certainty in his tone.

He presses a kiss to my hair, lingering, his presence both commanding and tender. "Always," he whispers. "Aligned. Together. Nothing else matters. Not the contracts, not the chaos, not the world outside these walls. Only this. Only us."

I let myself settle fully into the embrace, into the calm certainty, into the quiet warmth of him holding me. "Only us," I echo, letting the phrase become a mantra for the day ahead.

We stay like that a while longer, neither of us speaking, just existing in the quiet intimacy of the room. The tension that had always defined us. The dark pull, the thrill of control and surrender is still there, but softened, tempered by trust and love.

Eventually, we rise slowly, moving together, sharing silent smiles and quiet gestures that speak louder than words. Even in the mundane morning, dressing, moving around the room, preparing for the day, we carried that closeness, that connection, that unspoken understanding.

Before long, I found myself at the door, the chaos of the day still looming but manageable, softened by the certainty that we faced it together. His hand rested lightly on mine.

"You ready?" he asked softly, voice low but firm, pulling me into his side once more.

"For today?" I asked, letting my lips curl into a small smile. "Always. With you."

He presses a gentle kiss to my temple, lingering just long enough to remind me of the bond we share. "Then let's go," he says. "Step by step. Together."

And in that moment, with the world beginning to stir outside our window, I felt it—our connection. I was under his spell, yes, drawn to him, captivated by his calm authority, but I was also free. Free to trust, free to love, and free to know that no matter what came next, we had each other.

And that made all the difference

CHAPTER 30

Gabe

IN THE KITCHEN ROSIE stood barefoot on the cold tile, the echo of her heels from the night before long gone. Her hair was no longer tousled, instead a long mahogany braid hung across her shoulder and sat between her breasts. The espresso machine hissed, and the smell of coffee filled the room.

I lean against the counter, arms folded. "So, now is all business...already, huh?" My voice is still rough from last night.

"Back to business," she says. "You know, there was a time I didn't want this. I didn't think I could do it." She sighs heavily. "I changed who I was to suit everyone else, but now...now, I know I can do it. With you by my side."

Looking at her here in the kitchen, I know this is the Rosie I met. Vulnerable. But I see in her eyes she is who everyone else here knows her to be...La Madrina.

She slides a steaming cup across the counter, and our fingers brush, just that simple touch sending a spark through us. I catch a trace of a smile on her lips, but as quick as a heartbeat, it's gone.

"What?" she asks.

"Just enjoying the view." My tone is casual, but I keep my eyes on her, just searching. "You got that storm brewing again."

She doesn't deny it. She can't.

Last night she let go. It turns out I am now the only one who gets to see the woman beneath the title. But the sunrise always brings the job back. The empire doesn't run itself.

"Come on," she says, setting the cup down. "There's work to do."

The walk to her office is short, and I feel the air change with every step. Any warmth from the kitchen vanishes, replaced by something colder. Rosie opens the door, the scent hitting first...iron and smoke. Two bodies lay sprawled on the floor, Massimo and Enzo. Men who, according to Rosie, served their purpose, but she didn't trust them.

She steps over the corpses like they are trash waiting for collection. The blood on the marble has dried to a dull rust color. I follow her inside, watching as she sinks into her chair. The high-backed leather one behind the desk.

She glances up at me. "Close the door."

I obey. Always.

For a long moment, the only sound is the ticking of the clock on the wall.

"I need to call Nico," she says finally.

I only nod in response. I know this must happen but not knowing what the outcome will be.

Picking up the phone she dials. It only rings twice before the deep voice on the other end answers.

"Nico."

"Rosie," he responds.

"I need a favor."

I don't hear anything. I feel my heart beating, waiting for him to respond to her. "That depends."

"Tommy. I want him here today to remove two bodies. I would have asked last night, but I felt it was best to let things settle."

"I already have him on standby."

Her voice is steady. "Perfect, send him over."

I watch her as she speaks, her hand loose around the receiver and eyes fixed on the painting on the wall. The woman who'd been soft in my arms last night is gone, this is the version the underworld fears, the one who doesn't flinch.

Nico sighs. "You're lucky I like you. Tommy will handle it. But the meeting, my place. NIC building, financial district. Marco's sitting in."

Her jaw flexes. It appears this version of Rosie hates being told where to go, who to face. "Fine," she tells him. "See you there."

Hanging up, she leans back, exhaling through her nose. For the first time that morning, fatigue flickers across her features.

I come closer, resting my hands on the edge of the desk. "You're letting him set the stage?"

"It's strategic."

"Feels like a concession."

She looks up at me, her eyes narrowing. "You questioning me, Gabe?"

I meet her gaze, unflinching. "Never. Just reminding you who you are. He may be my brother and we may be friends, but don't let him take advantage of that."

That earns the faintest smirk. "Trust me, I remember."

I nod, glancing at the bodies again. "And the rest of your people, they'll fall in line after this?"

"They'll fall in line," she says. "But I need someone at my right-hand I can trust. Someone who won't blink."

For a heartbeat, her eyes linger on me. We both know what that look means and what she can't have. I am Nico's second. A line we can't cross without lighting the city on fire.

I look away first. "You'll find someone."

"I'll have to." Standing, she smooths her tight-fitting pencil skirt as if two dead bodies weren't still in the room. "Get rid of these," she says quietly. "Before Tommy gets here. I don't want his men seeing too much."

I smile as she has no issues with me being in here but hates the idea of anyone else, yet I am Nico's second. I bend down, grabbing one of the men by the collar, dragging him toward the side door that leads to the freight elevator. Rosie watches me as I remove the men one by one, her mind already spinning through names of men who could replace the dead, who she could trust to hold the line.

When I return, she is standing by the window again, arms folded, the rose garden sprawled out in front of her.

"Nico and Marco won't like that you handled this yourself," I say. "They'll see it as reckless."

She turns, and for a moment her expression softens. "They'll see it as necessary. And that's enough." Her eyes narrow as she glances at me. "Come with me to the meeting," she says finally.

"You sure?"

"I need someone who won't smile in their faces."

I smirk. "That I can do."

She nods once, decision made. "Good. We leave in an hour."

She walks past me toward the hall. By the time she reaches the door, the faint traces of warmth from earlier are gone, replaced by the chill authority of a woman who rules an empire built on fear and respect. I watch her go, knowing exactly what it means to love someone like her. She is fire and frost, one touch could save you or burn you to ash.

As we leave the mansion together, nothing is said about the night before or the bodies cooling in the basement.

We don't have to.

CHAPTER 31

Rosie

THE HUDSON GLEAMS BENEATH the morning sun as we step out of the car. The financial district is the kind of place where deals are made with a handshake and a knife in the back simultaneously.

Gabe walks beside me, his presence grounding, but I feel him tense. I know exactly what he's thinking. Keep quiet and don't intervene. The NIC building rises before us, glass and steel reflecting the city in fractured shards. I smooth my jacket, and reminded myself why I'm here. I'm not just a woman with power. I am La Madrina. And this meeting will make that clear.

Nico is waiting in the conference room, the same high-backed leather chair at the head of the table I'd come to recognize as a throne. He stands when we enter, a wide smile breaking across his face as he steps forward. Then he does something I hadn't expected, he pulls Gabe into a firm, brotherly hug.

"You look happy," Nico says, his voice warm but steady.

Gabe returns it, the ease between them unmistakable. I watch silently as Nico releases him and gestures toward the chairs. "Please, sit. Both of you."

Marco mirrors the gesture, stepping forward with a grin, hugging Gabe as well. Then he looks at me, and with the smallest incline of his head, shakes my hand. There is respect in his eyes. I am a player, and they know it.

I take my seat, heels crossing deliberately, letting my gaze sweep over the room. Nico and Marco's attention on me now. It is my move.

"I wanted to meet today," I begin, my voice measured and confident, "to make sure we're aligned. What I have, it's not just for me. It can be mutually beneficial."

Nico leans back slightly, nodding. "Go on."

"The casinos, the docks on the other side of the Hudson," I continue, watching every flicker in their eyes. "they run without interruption. No law enforcement interference, no unnecessary conflicts. The restaurants I've opened aren't just profitable, they can expand your footprint. Together we can run the East Side. All of it. Not just parts."

I let the words sink in. Power in silence. The room feels heavier, but I continue. "With the docks under both our families," I say, leaning forward, hands on the table, "we control what goes in and out. Nothing comes in without our say so. No exceptions."

Nico nods, absorbing the scope of my plan. Marco shifts in his chair, his eyes sharp, weighing my ambition. I see the calculation behind his smile, the mental math running.

I lean back, letting my heels tap lightly against the floor. “But…” I say, the single word heavy with meaning, “there’s one thing I need first. A second. Someone I trust completely. Someone who can operate seamlessly in my absence and enforce the standards I expect.”

There is a pause, and I feel every eye in the room, waiting for a response. Nico’s lips press together, and then…he looks over at Marco. My heart skips a beat.

“No,” I whisper under my breath, though everyone heard it. The tension tightens like a vice.

“You need someone you can trust,” Nico says slowly, voice smooth and controlled. “Rosie, when I first met you, I learned to trust you, then, as you know, we had this small matter of well…this.” He gestures between us, and I know he is talking about the contract marriage. I broke his trust by dealing with everything on my own. I called Harridan, like always, when Frankie would have helped and so would Nico. I look back toward him and he finishes.

“But now we need to learn to trust each other. And that starts today.”

Gabe’s hand tightens around his coffee cup, and Marco’s brow arches. I feel my stomach knot. The man Nico is suggesting as my second is no ordinary choice. Gabe shifts beside me, his posture stiff, eyes locked on me. I feel his disbelief, his silent protest. But he doesn’t speak. He wouldn’t. Not here. Not now.

“I know what you’re thinking,” Nico continues, eyes steady, meeting mine. “Gabe is my second. My brother. That’s not changing. Whether you’re married or not, his position is secure. But the man I’m offering as your right-hand…he’s someone I trust implicitly. And now, you will, too.”

I take a slow breath, letting the words sink in. My empire needs structure. My people need leadership beyond me. But the weight of Nico's choice presses down on me like a weight on my chest. I would have to work with him. Trust him. Count on him when I wanted to trust only Gabe.

And Gabe... Gabe looks at me now, his jaw tight, eyes stormy. The fire in him, barely contained, mirrors the one I carry. I know exactly what he wants, to argue, to step forward, to say no. But he stays quiet, honoring boundaries he has no choice but to respect. And in that silence, I understand everything about what it meant to love him in this life.

I lean back, crossing my arms, a small smirk brushing my lips. "Fine," I say finally. "We'll do it your way. But make no mistake, I'll measure loyalty by results, not intentions."

Nico inclines his head, satisfied. "That's all I ask."

Marco exhales, shaking his head with a faint grin. "Rosie, you're ruthless, I'll give you that. It's...impressive."

I allow myself a fraction of satisfaction, a quiet triumph. This is my floor, my strategy, my plan. And yet, beneath it all, the ache of wanting Gabe to be not just here but beside me, unrestricted, whispers in the back of my mind. But he would stay. He will always stay. And I will rule this city, this side of the Hudson, with or without bending for him.

The meeting ends shortly after, handshakes exchanged, nods given, and respect silently acknowledged. As we step into the elevator, Gabe's hand brushes mine.

"You okay?" he asks, his voice low.

I look at him, letting the corner of my lips curve. “I'm better than okay. I'm in control. And for now...that's enough.”

He nods, but I can see it in his eyes, the frustration, the devotion, the part of him that wants to protect me from all of this. I reach for his hand briefly, letting him feel the truth he can't change. I don't need saving.

Not from Nico. Not from Marco. Not even from the city itself.

I am La Madrina. And nothing, not even the man I love was going to stop me.

CHAPTER 32

Marco

LEANING BACK AGAINST THE dark walnut edge of the conference table, my arms folded, jaw tight. The room is now quiet, the kind of quiet that only ever preceded decisions with consequences. Through the floor-to-ceiling windows, the city looked peaceful, it was a sunny day and the purist blue skies settled above us. Yet, despite the city's calm, tension hung heavy in the air.

I wasn't going to question Nico in front of Rosie, I would only agree, this is how we work, but I have to know. I look over at him sitting at the table, fingers steepled. I feel him studying me. That gaze, calm and precise. I can't flinch and definitely can't fucking stumble. Not today.

"So...why me?" I ask finally, my voice steady, but carrying the weight of genuine curiosity. "Why not Tommy? He's been a second before."

Nico doesn't respond immediately. Instead, he rests back in his chair, letting my question linger. He never answers right away when it matters, never rushes a conversation that requires thought, or manipulation, or both.

"This isn't about experience," he says finally. "It's about trust. And for too long, Marco, you've been concentrating on things that don't matter." His eyes glint with amusement. "The PA, for example."

I flex my jaw. I know exactly what Nico means. For months, I've been juggling responsibilities, patching holes, overseeing operations that weren't entirely mine. But I'd adapted. I'd thrived. But always under Nico's watchful eye, always aware that one misstep could shift the balance entirely.

"And she?" I say cautiously, referring to the woman who has upended the East Side, whose reputation has spread faster than anyone could anticipate. "She's...competent?"

Nico's laugh is low, almost cruel. "Competent isn't the word, Marco. She's calculated, smart, fearless, qualities you can't teach, qualities you either have or you don't. She has loyalty, yes, but more than that, she has vision. And I need someone like that aligned with her. Someone she trusts. Someone we can all trust."

I dip my brow. I had seen loyalty tested, allegiances shift, men who thought themselves untouchable swallowed by circumstance. But this...this felt different. I had always respected Nico's decisions, even the one where he shot my brother Tony. I stood by him even then.

"So why me?" I ask, a note of frustration in my voice. "Why not Tommy? He's proven. He knows how to follow orders. Knows the system."

Nico's eyes sharpen. "Because it's not just about following orders, Marco. It's about trust. And loyalty. You've always been loyal, yes, but your attention has been divided. Too long, focused on the wrong things." His tone softens only slightly, but the edge remained. "The PA, for example. Handling details while missing the bigger picture. That stops now. I'm giving you clarity. And responsibility."

I exhale, the weight of it settling in my chest. Responsibility wasn't new. Leadership wasn't new. But Nico's words carried a subtle warning, step wrong and the consequences wouldn't be minor. They never were with Nico.

"The PA has to go, she isn't up to the job, Nico, I keep telling you this?" My voice is tired having repeated this over and over. I can't work with her, she is a distraction I didn't need, and now...now it's even more important she isn't here.

Nico slams his fist on the desk, the sound reverberating through the office, sharp enough to make me flinch. "She is not leaving!" he barks. "She will not be a distraction. If she becomes one, if this carries on, and you don't deal with it, then I will. And you won't like my way."

My heart thuds. Nico's wrath is precise and equally terrifying.

I straighten, inhaling deeply. "I understand. Completely." I had no choice but to agree. This was about loyalty, proof that I could handle what was coming. That I could manage the balance between Nico's expectations, Rosie's ambition, and my own instincts.

Nico leans forward, eyes blazing. "And Marco...deal with your personal hesitation. Stop hiding behind excuses and fuck her already. She will not be a distraction," Nico repeats, voice steady now, slicing through the tension like a blade. "If you allow your hesitation, your pride, or your fucking cock, to get in the way, then I will intervene. And I promise you, you won't fucking like it."

Inhaling, I feel my chest tighten. Nico didn't joke. He never joked about loyalty or authority. He never joked about the consequences. I exhale slowly, letting the words sink in.

I lean against the edge of the desk, silent, thinking. Loyalty. Trust. Execution. Words I had been following for years, yet today they carried a heavier meaning. I was no longer just a capo. I was the bridge between the Romanos' and Contis' rising empire. Every choice mattered. Every hesitation could be fatal.

Glancing out of the window at the Hudson below, the docks, the traffic, the heartbeat of New York. I thought about the men, the operations, the delicate web of alliances and power that Nico had built, and the new thread now woven with Rosie. I understood, finally, what Nico had been saying all along. Trust wasn't blind. Loyalty wasn't given lightly. And execution wasn't just doing the job. Execution was carrying the weight of the empire, every consequence, every decision, every human factor, and making it work without letting it break you. Nico's hand rested lightly on the table, watching me, a predator waiting for affirmation.

I nod slowly. "I'll handle it. I won't let you...or her...down."

"That's what I thought," Nico says, his voice deadly calm.

For the first time in weeks, I feel a spark of clarity. Nico's choice was not just about Rosie. It was about me, about proving I could carry responsibility, control desire, and honor the chain of command without bending the rules. And for the first time, I knew I could.

CHAPTER 33

Rosie

MY HOME OFFICE SMELLED faintly of coffee, the organized chaos of operations in full view. I had ledgers stacked, maps of the city pinned to the walls, notes in my handwriting everywhere. Marco stood by the doors, arms crossed, looking into the garden.

I gesture toward the chairs. "Sit," I tell him. "We've got work to do."

He obeys, carefully folding himself into the chair across from mine. I study him for a moment, letting the silence stretch. There is an edge to him, the kind of edge you could only earn by surviving in the middle of a war of families. And now, he is stepping into my world. My empire.

"Let's start with the restaurants," I say finally, pulling a folder from the stack in front of me. The photos, receipts, and delivery schedules are neatly arranged, color-coded for clarity. "We need to ensure deliveries come in cleanly, efficiently. No delays, no mistakes. The capos will oversee this side of things. You can introduce yourself to them and explain how you'll handle it."

He nods in agreement. "Consider it done. I'll go through the schedules, the routes, and make sure the men understand the chain of command. I'll take responsibility for this entirely. No mistakes, no excuses."

I allow a small smile. "Good. I trust that you're comfortable with that. I want this relationship, between us, our operations...to be smooth."

He raises an eyebrow, a faint smirk tugging at his lips. "I can work like that. Clear lines. Respect. Authority. It's not difficult when you know your role."

"Exactly," I agree. "Now, the casinos." I lean back in my chair, letting my eyes scan him. "This is where we clean the money. Large sums move through these rooms. I need to know that the process will be seamless. That nothing will slip."

"I'll oversee it," Marco says. "I'll make sure the men are following protocol. There's no room for error, Rosie. Not here."

I nod, satisfied. "Good. And the docks?" My voice drops slightly, more deliberate. "You'll need to introduce yourself to my men there. Go through which routes will now be used legitimately. Make sure everyone knows who reports to whom. I don't want any confusion. Nothing leaves or enters without proper authorization. Our empire is only as strong as the weakest link."

Leaning back in his chair, his thumb and forefinger rub across his stubble. "Understood. I'll make the introductions, explain the routes, and ensure compliance. You have my word."

I study him, letting my gaze linger. I sense his trust, in the way he spoke, he's competent and I see his loyalty.

"I want this relationship to work," I say finally, voice low but firm. "I trust you're happy with this, Marco. That you're comfortable in this role."

"I am," he tells me, meeting my eyes. "I know what I need to do. And I'll do it."

The tension between us eases slightly, replaced by a shared understanding. We aren't friends. Not yet. But for the first time, I felt a sense of alignment, our goals, our authority, and our respect for one another all moving in the same direction.

I let out a slow breath and lean back, crossing my legs. "Good. Then we move forward."

Before either of us could speak again, the office door clicked open. Harridan stepped in, tall and imposing, with her usual air of arrogance. Her eyes swept over the room, landing on me.

"Rosie," she greets, her voice firm, but with just the hint of urgency that always made me pay attention. "I need a favor."

I raise an eyebrow at her, letting the words hang in the air. Marco shifts slightly, watching how I handle this new interruption.

"Go on," I say, leaning forward slightly. "Tell me what it is."

Her gaze sharpens. "It's delicate."

"Alright," I say finally. "Let's hear it."

CHAPTER 34

Rosie

AS SOON AS HARRIDAN said she needed to speak in private, I knew this wasn't business. Not the usual kind, anyway. There was a glint of mischief in her eye, that only ever meant trouble disguised as a favor.

"Marco," I say, glancing toward him. "Give us a minute."

He stands, nodding respectfully. "Of course. I'll get started on what we discussed."

There it is again, that small, silent acknowledgment. A man who understood rank, who knew how to move in a room without challenging it. He inclined his head, and for a split second, it almost looked like he bowed before turning and walking out. The door clicking shut behind him.

Harridan waits until she is sure we are alone before she jumps to her feet and claps her hands together, grinning. "Finally!" she says, eyes wide with excitement.

"You're where you belong, Rosie. You *own* this room. Did you see the way he basically bowed when he left? Boss bitch energy!" Her infectious laughter fills the office.

I can't help it, the corner of my mouth curves upward, and before I know it, I'm smiling, really smiling. The kind that comes when you're too tired to pretend you're made of stone. I lean back in my chair, feeling the tension start to drain out of me.

"Alright, alright," I say, chuckling softly. "Spit it out. What's this favor?"

Harridan sits back down, still buzzing with that electric energy that always follows her into any room. "Okay, so, you know Shank's birthday is coming up..."

I raise an eyebrow. "The Soul Reapers President?"

She nods. "Yeah. You know how everyone in that club loves their bikes, chrome, engines, noise, the works? Well, he's been talking non fucking stop about the 1977 Triumph Bonneville Silver Jubilee. Limited run, only available in the UK, total fucking classic. And guess who found one?" She jabs her thumb at her chest, grinning like a kid in a candy shop.

I laugh. "You didn't?"

"Oh, I fucking *did*." Her grin widens. "But here's the problem. I need to get it over here, and I don't have time for all the customs shit. The paperwork, the inspections, the waiting, it'll never make it in time."

I tilt my head, smirking. "So, you're asking me to smuggle a vintage motorcycle across the Atlantic?"

"'Smuggle' is such an ugly word," she says with a mock gasp. "Let's call it...*expedited importing*. You're good at that, right?"

I shake my head, still smiling. "You're unbelievable."

Her eyes sparkle with mischief. "If I get the guy to deliver it to Dover, can you help me get here?"

I sigh, but the smile never leaves my face. Harridan is my weakness, the one person who could walk into my empire and talk to me like I was still the girl in the children's home before all this power.

"Fine," I say finally, pretending to sound exasperated. "I'll help you. But I'm not taking a dime for it."

Her grin falters. "Rosie-"

I raise my hand, cutting her off. "No. You're my ride or die, Harridan. I'm here today because of you. You've had my back from day one. I don't forget things like that."

She opens her mouth to protest again, then just sighs and nods. "Alright, boss or should I say La Madrina. No payment. But you're making me look bad with all this fucking generosity."

I chuckle. "You'll survive." Leaning across the desk, I pull a small notepad closer and scribble a number, tearing the page cleanly before handing it over. "Here, call Marco, he'll handle the logistics. Once it arrives, he'll get in touch."

She looks down at the paper, then back up at me, eyebrows raised. "The guy that just left the room? The new second?"

I nod. "Yeah. He's good. Efficient. You can trust him."

She smirks at me, slipping the paper into her jacket pocket. "You sound like you already do."

I give her a look, half amused, half warning. "Don't start."

I stand and walk to the doors, staring out at the rose garden. It always looked so peaceful, but I knew better. Peace was just the quiet before the next storm.

"Thanks, Rosie," Harridan says, softer now. "You've got enough on your plate, and you still find time for the people who matter."

I turn, meeting her eyes. "That's the point, isn't it? Power doesn't mean anything if you forget where you came from, besides you've always been there for me."

She smiles at that, a real smile, warm and proud. "You've changed, you know. But not in the way I expected. Your sharper, colder maybe, but you still have a heart under all that iron."

"Don't tell anyone," I say, a small grin tugging at my lips. "I've got a reputation to maintain."

Harridan laughs and stands, heading for the door. "Your secret's safe with me, La Madrina."

As the door shuts behind her, I sink back into my chair, staring at the fading light over the garden. For the first time in a long time, I allow myself to just *breathe*.

This world was built on loyalty, blood, and power. But moments like this? They remind me why I am here. At first, I was proving a point to Teddy, but now, I am going to build this empire bigger than he ever did.

But for now, I allow myself the rarest luxury of all. A moment of peace.

CHAPTER 35

Gabe

THE HOUSEKEEPER MEETS ME at the door before I've even finished shrugging off my jacket. Her voice is soft but formal, trained by years of working under powerful people.

"Mr. Romano," she says with a polite nod. "Supper is being served in the dining room."

"Thanks," I murmur, adjusting my cuffs as I step inside.

The house is quiet, too quiet for a place this big. The marble floors and high ceilings make every footstep echo. The Contis' place had always felt old. When I arrived, it was obvious that Rosie had gutted pretty much every room in the place. She's trying to make it hers. And now, maybe, ours.

When I reach the dining room, she is already there. Rosie sits at the far end of the long oak table, a small smile tugging at her lips. Two places are set, silver cutlery, crystal glasses, candlelight flickering in the reflection of the dark windows.

"Gabe," she greets softly. "Sit."

I do.

She glances at the staff, then lifts a hand. "Leave us."

They move silently, clearing out until the only sound left is the ticking from the grandfather clock in the far corner of the room.

Her eyes follow me for a moment before she speaks. "We have things to discuss."

Something in her tone has me swallowing. With Rosie, that phrase could mean anything now, strategy, territory, or something that would upend my carefully balanced world.

I clear my throat. "Should I be worried?"

Her chuckle is low and genuine. "No," she says, eyes sparkling. "Not this time."

I raise an eyebrow. "That's reassuring."

She leans back in her chair, letting her fingers trace the rim of her wine glass. "We need to redecorate," she states matter-of-factly. "This house...this shell, needs to become our home."

For a moment, I just blink. Of all the things she could've said, that wasn't what I expected.

She continues before I can answer. "This arrangement may not have you here with me as much as I'd like," she says softly, "but it's still ours. I want us to be comfortable here."

I can't help but laugh, the tension breaking a little. "So, what, you want us to go to Target together and pick out soft furnishings?"

Her eyes flash with amusement, and for a second, the queen disappears and there is just Rosie, the woman who could still make me laugh in the middle of all this madness.

"Not quite," she says with a grin. "I have someone coming tomorrow. A designer. We can tell them what we want."

"What *you* want, you mean," I tease.

She tilts her head. "No, Gabe. What *we* want. You live here too."

The word hits harder than I expected. *We.* I'd spent years standing behind my brother Nico, behind the family name, always the soldier, the strategist, never the man allowed to choose softness. But Rosie...she made space for it. For me.

She pours me a glass of wine and passes it across the table. "You'll need an office here," she tells me, changing the subject as easily as she commands a room. "You don't want to travel into the city every day...do you?"

I take the glass, smiling faintly. "You really think Nico's going to let me work out of a home office?"

Her smirk is sharp, knowing. "Let me worry about Nico."

Leaning back in my chair, I watch her. The candlelight catches the edge of her face, softening what the world called La Madrina, and highlighting my angel.

"You've been running nonstop," I say quietly. "You don't need to add redecorating to the list."

Shaking her head. "This isn't about redecorating. It's about control. About building something that belongs to us, not just the business." Her eyes soften, just a fraction. "This house has seen too many ghosts. It's time it starts seeing something better."

I don't say anything for a while. I just look at the woman who has killed to protect her empire, who could stare down Nico Romano without blinking, who could make me feel both proud and helpless in the same breath.

Finally, I nod. “Alright. We’ll do it your way.”

Her lips curve. “My way is usually the right one.”

I chuckle. “I’ve noticed.”

For a few minutes, we eat in silence. She reaches across the table, fingers brushing against mine. “Thank you, Gabe,” she says softly.

“For what?”

“For being here.”

I squeeze her hand once before letting go. “Always,” I say.

And I mean it.

CHAPTER 36

Rosie

THE HOUSE FINALLY FELT alive. For months now, we'd worked to turn it from a shell of marble and silence into something that felt like ours, mine and Gabe's. The walls no longer echoed. Flowers bloomed in the hallway. Candles burned low in the corner of the dining room. The scent of garlic and rosemary drifted from the kitchen. I was setting the last of the wine glasses when the front door flew open.

"Rosie!"

Before I could even turn, Frankie came barreling through like she owned the place, arms wide and grin unstoppable. She wrapped me in a hug that nearly lifted me off my feet.

"Fuck!" she says, holding me at arm's length. "Look at you. You look like the queen you always were, but she was hiding underneath for a while."

I couldn't help but laugh. "You're ridiculous."

She flicks her hair back dramatically. "Maybe. But I'd like to take some of the credit, thank you very much." She winks, and I laugh harder.

Behind her, Nico steps into the room with that unhurried confidence that always filled whatever space he enters. Gabe follows, sleeves rolled up, looking perfectly at home in this new version of our world.

Nico's handshake is firm, but no longer businesslike. "The place looks good," he says, glancing around. "Feels...homey."

"That was the goal," I tell him. "We needed something that wasn't just a place to sleep between wars."

He chuckles, then gestures for us all to sit. Gabe starts to pour the wine. For a moment, it almost feels like an ordinary evening.

Almost.

Once dinner has been served and conversation begins to flow, Nico's tone shifts. Business always found him, even at a dinner table.

"The ports are running smoothly," he states, slicing through his steak with precise movements. "Everything moving through customs without so much as a second look. And the casinos...flawless. No issues."

I nod, taking a slow sip of wine. "Marco's been working hard. He managed to transfer fifty percent of the operations into legitimate fronts last week. We're on track to be fully clean by the end of the year."

Nico grunts approvingly. "Good. It's cleaner this way. Fewer cracks for outsiders to crawl through."

Before I can respond, Frankie puts her fork down and rolls her eyes. "Oh, please. That's not what we're here for."

Nico shoots her a look. "Frankie..."

She waves him off. "No. We're family. This isn't some boardroom meeting. Tonight's about celebrating what we've built. What we *are* building." She turns to me with a grin. "You've done something incredible, Rosie. You've turned chaos into structure, and I'm proud of you. But what we *should* be talking about is Marco and his PA."

I blink. "Excuse me?"

She leans forward, eyes gleaming with mischief. "You heard me. Has he fucked her yet?"

Across the table, Gabe nearly chokes on his drink while Nico's fork freezes midair.

"Frankie," he says, voice low, dangerous.

"What?" she exclaims innocently, holding up her hands. "It's a fair question! You're all thinking it."

"I'm *not*," I say sharply, though the corner of my mouth twitches in amusement.

Nico's tone hardened. "If his personal life starts to interfere with business, I'll remove the fucking problem, he knows this."

The air in the room shifts. The warmth evaporating, replaced by something colder.

I set my glass down carefully and look straight at him. "He's my second, and I'll take care of my own affairs," I tell him evenly.

He meets my stare, a brief spark of challenge, old habits resurfacing but then he nods once, curt and accepting. He respects strength, he always had.

Gabe, sensing the tension, leans back in his chair and lets out a low chuckle. "Business can wait." His voice is calm but firm. "What we have here, this right now, is what matters most. Family."

Frankie smiles, satisfied. "Hell yeah."

I exhale slowly, raising my glass. "To family."

Nico's expression softens, lifting his glass too. "To family."

All our glasses clink, the crystal ringing through the air.

The conversation drifts back to easier things, Frankie teasing Gabe about the new decor, Nico grumbling about the designer's color choices, laughter finding its way back into the room. And for that moment, surrounded by people who had fought, bled, and built with me, I allowed myself to feel something rare...comfort.

It wouldn't last. It never did in our world. But for tonight, it was enough.

Chapter 37

Gabe

DINNER HAD SETTLED INTO that easy rhythm. Laughter over wine, Frankie teasing Nico until he was half growling, half smiling, and Rosie looking every inch the queen she'd become. She had this calm now. Not just the kind that came from peace, she'd never have that fully, but from control. Everything in her world was running how she wanted it. Until the door opens fast, Marco stepping inside, chest heaving slightly. His eyes flick across the table, looking at Nico, Frankie, and me before landing on Rosie.

I see it in him instantly...conflict. Duty pulling him one way, instinct another. He goes straight to her, leaning down and whispering something quietly into her ear.

Her expression doesn't change. She simply nods once before pushing her chair back. "Excuse me," she tells us all smoothly. "Please, continue." She stands, placing her napkin on the table, a faint smile appearing on her lips as she glances across to me before leaving the room. Marco follows her without another word. The door closes softly behind them.

Nico lets out a growl and tosses his napkin onto the table. "What the fuck was that about?"

I shrug, keeping my tone even. "How the fuck should I know. Rosie and I..." I pause, meeting his stare. "We don't discuss business. You know that."

He grunts, clearly irritated but knowing I am not lying. Then Nico's phone chimes. Picking it up, he glances at the screen and swears under his breath.

I stand immediately, stepping around the table. "What is it?"

He turns the phone so I can see the message...Tony.

"The club's being raided," Nico hisses. "The IRS is there with the FBI. They're demanding the books."

I clench my jaw. "The *FBI*? Why the fuck are they involved?"

Frankie freezes, her glass halfway to her lips. "That's not just tax trouble, Nico."

He nods grimly. "No. It's a message."

"I'll make some calls," I tell him, already pulling my phone from my pocket. We have people everywhere, city hall, customs, in departments that pretend to regulate us. You don't survive in this world without them. Before I can dial, the door opens again.

Rosie walks back in like nothing happened, calm and collected. Her dress catches the light as she moves, a walking angel.

She smiles faintly at the table. "Nico," she says evenly, "there's been a leak in the ranks. One of the soldiers, most likely. Marco has already sent for the one we suspect."

I look over to Nico and watch as he leans back in the chair, his eyes narrowing. "And *my* club?"

"Raided," she responds simply.

"Yes, I know," he responds.

She nods knowingly and takes her seat gracefully. "It's handled."

The silence that follows is thick, the kind that only comes when violence hovers just out of reach.

Nico's phone chimes again. He looks at the screen and smiles. "Seems you do have everything under control," he tells her as he sets the phone back down.

Rosie lifts her glass and doesn't break eye contact. "I do. They won't be back. And even if they are, Marco's made sure there's nothing to find." Taking a sip of her drink, her eyes meet mine for just a second, and there it is again, that unspoken thing between us.

Trust.

Nico laughs softly, shaking his head. "I'll never understand how you stay that calm."

Rosie smiles faintly. "Because panic never solved anything."

Frankie exhales and mutters, "Well, that was a fucking buzzkill," before taking a gulp of her wine.

I stay standing, my phone still in my hand, just watching Rosie. The queen of composure, sitting in her house, *our* house, steady in the storm. And I think to myself, not for the first time, that if anyone ever went against her, FBI, IRS, fuck, even Nico, they wouldn't just lose. They'd vanish.

CHAPTER 38

Rosie

THE PLATES WERE NEARLY empty, glasses half-drained, the buzz of wine and laughter softening what had been a tense evening. The air felt lighter now or maybe that was just an illusion. In our world, peace never lasted more than a few minutes at a time.

The dining room door opens again and Marco enters. He seems more put together this time, but the look on his face tells me everything.

"My apologies for the interruption, La Madrina," he says formally. "Luciano has arrived."

Placing my napkin on the table neatly, I acknowledge him. "Thank you, Marco." Then I looked back at the others. "It's been a lovely evening," I tell them with a faint smile. "But if you'll excuse me, I have something I must deal with."

When I stand, Gabe and Nico both follow...out of respect or out of instinct? Who knows?

Nico frowns, irritation flickering across his face. "I think I should help with this," he says, his voice short. "It was *my* club that got raided."

Turning toward him, a small smirk catching the edge of my lips. "It may have been *your* club, but Luciano is *one of my men.* You can come, Nico. But let's be clear...I'll decide how this ends."

For a second, the room is still. The challenge hung between us. Then Nico nods, not agreement exactly but acceptance.

He looks over to Gabe. "Make sure Frankie gets home safe."

Frankie bolts up from her chair, its legs scraping across the floor, folding her arms. "Fuck no. If you're all fucking going, I'm not missing out on this." Her scowl is almost comical, but there is steel behind it. If there's one thing Frankie loves, it's the kill.

I reach up and put my hand on my neck, moving it side to side until I hear the satisfying crack. I turn to Marco. "Escort Luciano to the basement, we'll be along shortly."

He nods once and leaves. The door closes and I face the others again, all three of them returning my gaze. Nico, Gabe, Frankie...my family.

"Look," I begin, my voice steady, carrying the authority I no longer have to fake. "It wasn't that long ago I was a shadow, keeping to myself, running from this life. But it found me again. And despite how hard I fought it...I know now I was made for this." The words came out low, but each one carries the truth that lives deep in my bones.

I step closer to them, maintaining eye contact. "Come if you want, but don't be mistaken. When we walk into that basement, *I* will be the one in control. And if any of you think otherwise..." I gesture toward the table, toward the empty glasses and half-eaten food. "Then take a seat. Or leave."

Silence follows my ultimatum. Frankie smirks, respect shining in her eyes. Nico doesn't say a word, but his jaw flexes, and Gabe...well, he just watches me, eyes unreadable. I don't bother to wait for their answer, just turn and leave the dining room.

The further I go, the darker it gets. The warmth of the house fades behind me, replaced by the cold stillness that always lived in the lower halls. The air smells faintly of metal and damp concrete. The door to the basement is already unlocked. I push it open, the old hinges groaning. The narrow staircase is uneven, worn from years of use. The dim bulbs hanging from rusted fixtures cast weak circles of light along the walls, barely cutting through the shadows. Pipes run along the ceiling, dripping occasionally, the sound echoing faintly in the silence.

At the bottom of the stairs, the space opens into a wide concrete room. There are old hooks along one wall, a single steel table in the corner, and in the middle of the room stands Luciano. He faces the door, hands fidgeting, sweat slicking his temple. When he sees me, he tries to straighten his posture, but his eyes give him away. Like a deer caught in headlights, they are wide, and he looks everywhere but at me. Already guilty.

I take my time crossing the floor, the sound of my heels echoing off the walls. "Ah, Luciano," I say softly, stopping just a few feet away from him. "You know, for a man with *loose lips,* you're awfully quiet tonight."

He swallows hard, eyes dropping to the floor.

I smile faintly, but it doesn't reach my eyes. "Good. Because I'm not in the mood for stories. I'm in the mood for the truth."

Behind me, I hear footsteps on the stairs, the others following, just like I knew they would. Nico's heavy steps, Frankie's lighter ones, and Gabe's steady pace. But this is my room. My rules.

And tonight, I intend to remind them all why they call me La Madrina.

CHAPTER 39

Rosie

I CIRCLE LUCIANO, SHOULDERS slumped, eyes darting between us. He is a weak man, no fight left in him, but I haven't started yet, this is just the realization of what doubt costs in our world. How have we had a man so weak that all it's taken to defeat him is the silence of a room? Pathetic.

"Who did you speak to?" I ask.

His eyes drift across to Nico, then go between Gabe and Marco before he answers, but he doesn't give me the answer, he responds to them. "Boss, listen, I had no choice...this woman came in from the FBI—" he rushes out, but I step forward striking his face.

"They didn't ask you anything," I hiss, his cheek glowing red with my handprint.

"Wh-what?" he stutters.

"I asked you a question, and you *will* address me." I take his face in my hand and pull it toward mine. "Do I make myself clear?"

"Yes, ma'am."

I see the shock on his face, not expecting this, but now I understand the root of our problem.

"Yes, who?"

I watch as he swallows, his Adam's apple bobbing up and down. "Yes, La Madrina."

Straightening my back, I drop my hands and nod for him to proceed.

"Err, well, this woman came in and at first we didn't know who she was, and we kinda got friendly...if ya know what I mean." A cocky grin fills his face.

This man is testing my patience. "Marco," I say, and gesture to the man in front of me, and with one look he strides over and punches him clean off the chair we'd given him. Blood gushes from his nose, making a mess everywhere; another job we will have to clean up because of this imbecile.

"What did I tell you about not wanting a story? Get to it," I demand, raising my voice. I don't know what it'll take for these men to understand that I am not going to take any shit from them...but they will soon learn.

"Okay, okay, I am sorry. I let slip...you know, we weren't all legit." He groans in pain. "I was trying to impress her."

"What else?" There is more, it is in his eyes.

The extent of his disloyalty is deeper than this. It may have been because he wanted to brag to some woman, but this wasn't all this snake had done. What I do know is that tonight won't be the night I find out. He has said all he is going to. He may have broken easily but I can see in his eyes that no matter what we do to him now, he will keep his lips sealed, because he knows he will not live to see the sun rise, no matter what he tells us.

I move closer to Luciano, my voice calm, almost kind. "You made a choice, Luciano. Your ego led you here, and after that you let doubt turn into disloyalty, and that spreads. I can't allow that."

He tries to speak, but no words will save him, not now.

"You were one of mine," I continue. "And I keep my house clean." The room is quiet, the others haven't spoken, and all I hear is the sound of the dripping pipes. I smile at him. "Oh, I won't kill you. I am not a murderer."

He exhales, the relief on his face plain to see.

I chuckle as Nico, Gabe, Marco, and Franco pull their weapons out and point them at the man in front of me, then tell him in unison, "I am."

"Oh...well, it's not looking good for you, is it Luciano?" I tell him as I walk away, heading back to the stairs. I lift my hand as my foot takes the first step. "End him."

Gun shots echo around the basement.

CHAPTER 40

Rosie

THE CASINO HUMS WITH the kind of life that only comes after midnight, dice clattering, dimes jingling against the metal, showcasing a winner. It looks like business as usual, but I know better. There's always something hiding under the noise.

Marco's already waiting by the back entrance near the surveillance room. His shirt sleeves are rolled up, tie loose, the kind of look that tells me he's been working too many hours and thinking too much.

"Marco," I greet, walking up beside him. "Tell me you've got something for me."

He nods once. "Your hunch was right. Luciano wasn't just running his mouth, he was running business behind our backs."

My jaw tightens. "Go on."

"He was letting some small-time gangs in," he tells me, glancing at the monitors where faces flickered in grainy black and white. "Selling dirty coke to gamblers in the bathroom corridors and even out by the valet line. Real subtle idiots. And not just here...the same thing was happening at two of the smaller casinos under your name."

The words hit like a punch in the stomach. I fold my arms. "And you handled it?"

"Mostly. But there's cleanup to finish."

Turning toward him fully. "Then double the men on the floors. I don't want a single packet of that garbage in my clubs or near my tables. The moment anyone sees a deal, they end it. You know how I feel about the cops sniffing around."

"Already on it." He nods in agreement.

"Good." I brush a stray hair from my face, glancing toward the main floor. "The casinos stay clean, no drugs. If anyone's going to make a mess, it'll be because I said so, not some backroom hustler thinking he can make a name for himself."

We walk into the main hallway together, the marble underfoot gleaming beneath the lights. As we reach the lobby, someone comes around the corner fast enough that they nearly run into me.

"Whoa—" The voice is all attitude...Marco's PA.

I tilt my head looking at her. "What are you doing here?"

This woman oozes confidence, and the way she flicks her hair over her shoulder like she is posing for the camera, almost makes me chuckle.

"Running *another* errand for Marco," she answers sweetly. "One of the *utmost* importance," she says sarcastically.

I arch my brow. "Is that right?" I turn to face Marco.

He shuffles slightly on his feet, immediately looking uncomfortable, which tells me everything I need to know.

Moving closer to him, I keep my voice low purposely. "Marco, why is she here? She's not supposed to be running your errands. That's what the soldiers are for."

Sighing, he rubs the back of his neck. "I know. I just..." He hesitates, his eyes flicking toward her retreating figure as she struts toward the exit. "I just wanted her out of the way."

I watch as his gaze follows her, seeing the telltale pull that's there, the conflict between duty and distraction. I understood that look. The heart is a liability in this world. The head is what keeps you alive.

Shaking my head, I wait until she is out of earshot, then turn back to him, keeping my tone even, but the warning is there. "Marco, your sex life is your business until it becomes mine. This..." I gestured around us, to the tables, the dealers, the empire we're building with the Romanos. "We can't afford blurred lines."

He looks down, working his jaw. "It's not like that, Rosie."

"Maybe not yet," I respond. "But I've seen how it starts. You care, then you protect, then you cover, and before you know it, loyalty's divided. You have to choose. If you want her in your life, then bring her all the way in. If not, keep her where she belongs, in the office, doing what she's paid to do."

His silence tells me he knows I am right.

I start to walk away, pausing to look back. "You're good at what you do, Marco. Don't let something small turn into something that knocks you off your game. We're too close to something big to get sloppy."

"You have my word, Rosie. I'll take care of it." He dips his head, acknowledging he understands what this means.

"I know you will, that's why you're here." I smile faintly.

I step into the elevator, the mirrored walls reflecting the faint neon glow from the casino. As the doors close softly, I catch one last glimpse of Marco watching me go, his shoulders squared again, but that flicker of uncertainty is still there.

Power isn't about being feared. It's about knowing where every weakness lies, even in the people you trust most. And tonight, I'd just seen his.

Chapter 41

Gabe

I HEARD HER VOICE before I saw her. Rosie's phone calls with Nico always sounded like that, short responses but straight to the point, yet oozing confidence, the kind that makes grown men sweat.

"The gangs at the club have been dealt with," she is saying as she walks through the front door, heels clicking against the marble. "The issue with the IRS looks like a one-off. Luciano ran his mouth trying to impress a woman...idiot move. Marco's already emailed the quarterlies." She stops mid-sentence when she sees me standing in the hallway. I didn't mean to startle her. I'd just come back from the gym downstairs, gray joggers, no shirt, skin still slick from the workout, but when her eyes find mine, they freeze like they've forgotten how to move.

"Yeah," she says into the phone, voice suddenly quieter. "We'll talk more tomorrow. Goodnight, Nico." She ends the call and slips the phone into her bag before it hits the floor with a soft thud as she crosses the space between us.

"Hard day at the office?" she asks, her tone half-teasing as she sucks in her bottom lip.

I smirk. "Hard day at the office," I tell her, stepping closer, pressing our bodies together. "And a hard day at home."

Her lips curve into that slow, dangerous smile that always made me forget where I ended and she began. "Your trouble, Romano."

"Only for you," I whisper and brush my thumb along her jawline.

She tilts her head slightly, eyes catching the faint light from the chandelier above. The power she carried all day, the woman who ordered men to clean up blood and balance books, I see it flicker behind her gaze. But right here, in this space between us, it softens.

Without saying anything more, I turn and walk toward the kitchen. I don't have to check if she is following. I feel her presence, the air shifting with every step she takes behind me.

The kitchen lights are low, the stainless steel catching the amber glow from the hallway and still smelling faintly of coffee and something sweet lingering in the air, her perfume. She leans casually against the doorframe, watching me as I grab a bottle of water from the fridge.

"You hungry?" she asks.

I twist the cap off, taking a sip, and look at her over the rim. "Starving," I say, my voice rougher than I meant it to be.

She smiles knowingly and crosses the room slowly, one deliberate step at a time. The sound of her heels on the tile matches the steady beat of my heart. When she reaches me, I catch her wrist, her pulse under my fingers steady but strong. She doesn't pull away.

"You shouldn't look at me like that," I tell her quietly.

"Like what?"

"Like you already know what I'm thinking."

"Maybe I do." Her tongue peeks out and traces her plump lips, leaving a glossy trail I want to follow. The air between us thickens. Her hand comes up to rest against my chest, her cool skin against my heat. "I missed you today," she murmurs.

"You were busy ruling the world," I say. "Didn't want to interrupt."

"I make time for what's important."

I lift her hand from my chest and press my lips to her knuckles. The smallest sound escapes her throat, half-breath, half-want, and it does something to me that words can't. The world has no idea what this woman is capable of, what she's already done to survive it. And yet here she is, standing in front of me in the half-light, softer than she ever let anyone see.

Setting the water bottle down, I close the distance between us, tracing a line down her arm until my fingers meet hers. "Rosie..."

She looks up at me, her eyes searching mine, and for a second, I see every version of her, the girl who used to hide, the woman who fought her way back, the queen who could silence a room with one word.

"Gabe," she whispers.

The rest doesn't need to be said.

The sound of her breath mixed with mine, the faint taste of salt and sweetness in the air, the press of warmth between us.

She leans into me, her voice barely a murmur against my skin. "You know what I like about you, Gabe?"

"What's that?"

"You never flinch."

"Not from you," I say. "Never from you."

The moment hangs there until she reaches up and kisses me, softly at first, then deeper like she is claiming me.

She had me from the minute I laid eyes on her, but this right here? This is mine. I think it's time La Madrina was reminded who is in charge when she's at home.

CHAPTER 42

Gabe

MY HAND GRASPS HER thick locks, pulling her mouth away from mine, feeling the warmth of her breath on my lips as our heads part.

"Gabe, please," she begs.

That's better, this is the Rosie I want when we're alone, the vulnerable, insatiable version, the one where I can see all her thoughts disappear, and I know all she is thinking about is this...us.

I tilt my head, moving closer to her neck, inhaling her sweet scent. "You look so fucking good begging for me."

I watch her pulse flutter so fast it is like watching a butterfly trying to escape from a cage. Ripping her silk cream blouse, I expose her lace bra, her nipples pebbling, teasing me from beneath the fabric. The buttons scatter against the tile floor, her chest rising and falling as she offers herself up to me, pushing her breasts toward me, brushing herself against my bare chest. Clenching my jaw, I spin her around, pushing her so her lower back knocks into the kitchen island. She smiles seductively as her eyes meet mine. I know what she's thinking. I love this side to her. Where she pushes boundaries and thinks she can take control. She likes to toy with me, both in and out of the bedroom.

Out of the bedroom, it works, she knows I cannot question her, and fuck its lead to many uncomfortable meetings, trust me. My cock knows what it wants and so does my heart.

In the bedroom, I don't have to hold back...unless I want to give her just a little taste of her own medicine, like now when she is looking at me like she believes one flutter of those chocolate brown eyes will break me.

I slide my fingertips up her arms and watch the goose pimples I leave in my wake. Her lips part as her breathy sighs get heavier. Discarding the remnants of her silk blouse, I yank down the cups of her lacy bra that have been hiding her luscious tits that are practically begging to be sucked. I purse my lips just imagining those hardening buds as my palm pushes her back on to the island, the coolness of the steel taking her breath away.

Unhooking her skirt, I pull it down, dropping it to the floor, leaving my angel in the barely there lace underwear she's been walking around in all day. A growl comes from deep inside, from want but also anger, bubbling up, knowing she's had this on all day with other men around her. Oh, I know they wouldn't get close enough to her to see, but my point remains that this underwear is for my eyes only, and I don't want to take any chances.

"You wore this to work?" I ask, but it's not really a question, more of a statement. I grip the side of her black lacy thong and yank hard, making her flinch. "You will only wear these when I am with you... Never when you're alone," I state.

Her eyes meet mine and I see the slight smile that catches the side of her mouth.

"I am not joking, Rosie, you don't want to test me. I have respected you outside of these walls, but if you disrespect me, then you will find out what happens." I hold her eyes and see the challenge there.

"We'll see," is all she says.

I chuckle as I know right now she doesn't believe me, but tonight I will make sure she understands. My hands stroke up her legs and dip inwards toward her pussy, holding her still as her body moves to get my hands where she truly wants them.

"Tomorrow, you will remember tonight. Every time you walk, sit, or stand, you will feel me." I smile as I step back and drop my joggers, revealing my long, hard cock. Moving closer, I take my throbbing cock, slick with pre-cum, and tease her already wet pussy.

"Please, Gabe. I need you," she begs. "Please."

It's like music to my ears, but it's not going to change anything yet. Ignoring her pleas, lifting her slightly so she feels the tip stretch her out...I know it's not enough, but that's all for now. I know how good fucking her velvety smooth pussy feels, but tonight, I want to fill her ass.

I want to own all of her...every single hole.

Spinning her around, my hand snakes between her thighs, gathering her juices and rubbing them against her asshole. Her sigh tells me all I need to know. She wants this, just as much as I do.

Kicking her legs wider, I drop to my knees and spread her cheeks with the palms of my hands. Sucking in, I look at the beauty laid out in front of me. "You look so fucking beautiful spread out for me," I tell her, my voice almost a whisper.

Leaning forward, I take a bite of her perfect ass cheek as she lets out a small squeal. I slap her ass as she moans with pleasure. My fingers tease her clit softly as I move forward and lick the entrance of her asshole. Her hips move back and forth, trying to get more pressure. She wants to come, I can sense it. Her legs start to shake, but this isn't how it's going to happen.

"Not yet, angel," I purr and move away, taking away the pleasure from her clit and ass.

She sighs loudly. "Gabe," she says desperately.

"It'll be worth the wait, angel. I promise." I slip my fingers back between her legs and start to tease her, and her body relaxes against mine. My fingers move back and push gently until they fit snugly into her tight asshole. Working one, then two fingers insider her, she starts to move back until she is fucking herself against me. I ease one more in until all the control I thought I had leaves me, and I line up behind her, replacing my fingers with my hard cock. Pushing gently, I ease my way in, my cock glistening with her juices as I watch it disappear into her ass inch by inch. I stand, fucking hard and fast, watching her cheeks bounce with each punishing thrust. Knowing we're close, I pull her closer, her back to my chest, and I grab her jaw, turning her head to face mine so I can watch her come undone for me. My other hand reaches around, feeling the wetness between her thighs, and teases her clit, rubbing faster, matching the rhythm of our thrusts.

Her sweet little cry is drowned out by my guttural moan as my seed fills up her ass. Her juices drip down my fingers as warm breath whispers across my face. As my cock slips out, I step back watching my cum drip down the inside of her thighs.

"I own every part of you, angel...including your heart."

Turning around, smiling sleepily, she nods. "You do."

CHAPTER 43

Rosie

STANDING BAREFOOT AT THE counter, the coffee cup steaming in my hand, my eyes drift to the kitchen island. The same polished surface where, just hours ago, Gabe had pressed me against cool metal and made the world fall apart in his arms. I trace a fingertip along the edge of the counter, the memories flooding back...his breath against my skin, the sound of him saying my name, the way I'd lost all control in a house that is now mine to command.

For once, there'd been no titles, no soldiers, no territory. Just us. The sound of my phone vibrating against the counter breaks through the haze. I turn the screen over. Marco.

I take a breath before answering. "Morning," I say, trying to sound casual.

His voice comes out rushed. "La Madrina, there's trouble at the casino."

His tone cuts through me faster than caffeine ever could. "What kind of trouble?"

"The gang's back," he tells me. "There were shots fired."

I put the mug on the counter a little harder than intended. "How bad?"

"Bad enough. The floor's clear now, but we need to move fast. I will come and get you."

I straighten, the last thoughts of warmth from the night disappearing under a familiar weight of focus. "No," I snap. "I'll meet you there. Handle what you can until I arrive."

He hesitates. "I should come to you first. We don't know who else is involved, and after what happened—"

"I said I'll meet you there." My tone leaves no room for debate.

There is silence on the line and then his quiet response, "Understood."

With nothing else to say, I cut the line. Behind me, I hear movement, bare feet on the tile and a low cough. I turn to see Gabe standing in the doorway, hair tousled, sweatpants hanging low on his hips. He looked too good for the chaos suddenly filling the room.

"What happened?" he asks, voice still gravelly from sleep.

"Marco called," I tell him, sliding my phone into my bag. "The gang's back. There were shots fired at the casino."

His jaw tightens, which makes my legs press gently together in response, thinking of the same action from last night. "Anyone hurt?"

Of course, I shake my head, bringing me back to the moment. "Not sure yet. He didn't say."

He grabs a T-shirt off the chair, pulling it over his head. "I'm driving."

"Gabe..."

He is already reaching for his keys. "Don't argue, Rosie. You know how this goes. If something's happening down there, I'm not letting you walk into it alone."

I sigh, but I don't fight him. He is right. He usually is when it came to keeping me alive. I slip on my jacket and follow him to the door.

Before we step out, he turns to me. "You ready?"

"Always," I say with a smile, then before logic catches up with me, I reach for his wrist and pull him in. The kiss is brief but heavy with everything words can't say, like thank you and be careful. "I love you," I whisper against his lips.

He smiles, that lazy, dangerous smile that ruined me from the start. "I know," he says softly. "And I love you too."

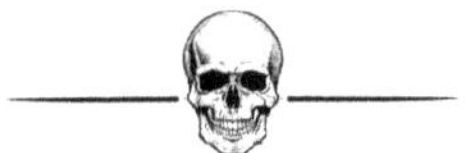

The drive through Jersey is quiet. The morning traffic blurs past, bridges and river light flashing through the windshield. Gabe's hand rests on the steering wheel, but his eyes keep flicking to me.

"What you thinking?" he asks finally.

"Isn't it supposed to be the woman who asks that?" I say with a chuckle.

"Now isn't the time for joking, Rosie."

Sighing, I roll my eyes...he's right. I look over at him. "Too much. Marco's voice, the word *shots*..." I shake my head. "The fact we just got everything under control and it's already slipping again."

He reaches over, brushing his thumb over my knee. "You'll fix it. You always do."

I just wish I could believe it was that simple.

By the time we reach the casino, the skyline is bleeding sunlight through clouds. The streets around the building are eerily empty, no crowds, nothing but the faint sound of sirens somewhere in the distance. Gabe parks near the back entrance, and we get out, scanning the area automatically.

Inside, the place wasn't right, it was too quiet. Casinos are never silent, they breathe noise. But now, even though the lights still blinked, and the machines kept spinning for no one, you can tell something is definitely off.

And there, in the middle of the main floor, stands Marco. He doesn't turn right away. He is staring down at something near his feet, a dark pool spreading slowly across the marble.

Blood.

"Marco," I call, "what is it?"

He looks up, face pale and eyes raw, and I know before he even speaks that something has gone wrong.

"She was here," he says, voice breaking slightly.

"She?"

He crouches and picks something up off the floor, a small black hair band. I can't see it properly, but he rolls it between his fingers so delicately.

"Marco..."

His jaw clenches. "My PA."

For a second, I can't speak, anger rising inside me, but I have to contain it. "She shouldn't have been here."

"I know." His voice is low, full of guilt. "I told her to collect the reports first thing." He stops, exhaling sharply. "I just needed her out of the way, just..." He doesn't finish.

Taking a slow breath, forcing the storm inside me to stay still. "We'll discuss this back at the office," I say finally. "Right now, I need to know what we're dealing with. What happened to the gang?"

"They're gone," he responds. "All of them. The soldiers got here before I did. It was over fast."

I scan the floor, eyes catching on the overturned chairs, the empty shell casings glinting near the bar. Too many signs of a fight that didn't need to happen.

"Any survivors?"

He shakes his head. "No one left to question, but the soldiers got one thing out of them before they dropped."

"What?"

He looks at me, eyes dark. "Luciano gave them the go-ahead. Told them the casinos were open ground for their product. They thought they had permission...from him."

The name feels like poison in my mouth. "But we took care of him?"

Marco nods. "Doesn't mean his ghost isn't still talking."

Gabe steps forward, his hand brushing my lower back, grounding me. "So, this whole mess started because of something Luciano set in motion before he was taken care of?"

"Looks that way," Marco says quietly.

I turn my gaze to the far side of the floor. Near the slot machines, a man is slumped sideways in a chair, lifeless, eyes open to nothing. His jacket is torn, stained with the same dark streaks as the floor.

"Who was in charge?" I ask, already knowing the answer before Marco points.

"That one," he says.

I nod slowly. Silence falls again. Only the low sound of the machines fills the air, spinning empty wheels that no one will ever cash out. The air smells like iron and spilled liquor, a scent I've known too long.

Marco is still holding the hair band, staring at it like it might tell him something. I watch the way his fingers tremble, small, barely there, but enough to see that this has cut deeper than he wants to admit.

"We'll find out what happened to her," I say softly.

He nods, but his eyes don't move from the floor.

Gabe shifts beside me. "What's your next move?"

I take one last look around the ruined casino. "We lock this down. Every entrance, every exit. No word gets out until we know who else was involved. If Luciano had people still loyal to him, they just made their last mistake."

I look back at Marco, meeting his eyes. I walk toward him and point at him "And you, you're going to make sure your head's clear before we do anything else. Whatever this thing is between you and that woman, you need to put it in a box and close the lid. You understand me?"

He hesitates, then nods. "Yeah. I understand."

"Good. Because the time for distractions is over." I turn toward the door, heading out to the morning light. Gabe beside me while Marco stays where he is, still holding that small, broken piece of someone who'd been too close to this life.

By the time we reach the front doors, I can already feel it, the shift, the tightening of power. The message has been sent. Whoever is left out there thinking I am a weakness in this world is about to learn otherwise.

As we step outside, Gabe's hand brushes mine. "You okay?" he asks quietly.

Looking up at him, my brows dip. "No," I tell him honestly. "But I will be."

Because everything I've worked for demands strength, and those that felt a woman doesn't have that would soon find out otherwise.

CHAPTER 44

Rosie

SITTING BEHIND THE GLASS walls of my office at NIC, just watching the morning light crawl across the city. Even from here, the casino disaster still burned in my mind's eye, the noise, the blood, the mess left behind. I liked it here at this time of the morning with only a few people in. It gives me time to concentrate. This is where I belong, behind glass, surrounded by order, turning chaos into structure.

At home, the office, even though I have changed it, still feels like his. No matter what I do, that man will always be a part of the room...killing him wasn't enough. Teddy will always plague my dreams; he made sure of that the day he took my mother from me. My mother's eyes will always be the last thing I remember of her, no matter how many photos I look at. I don't have time to think about that right now. I have to get to the bottom of what is going on this side of the Hudson. On the desk in front of me a dozen reports glow on my laptop. Numbers, camera feeds, name lists. It is all data until you learn to read between the lines. And I always did.

Luciano is dead, but trouble like his doesn't die easily, so it seems. It lingers—like a bad smell.

Clicking on a photo one of my men just sent from the casino floor, a new angle, zoomed in on the aftermath. The blood, overturned chairs, and one of the corpses lying slumped near the roulette wheels. I zoom in further...his face familiar. Then it hits me, the file Marco sent weeks ago with Luciano's background mentioned family. A brother, not much different in age.

Pulling up the file again, the resemblance is impossible to miss. Sitting back, I blow out a breath slowly. So, this wasn't just business. It was revenge. My phone is already in my hand before I've even finished the thought.

"Marco," I say when he answers.

"La Madrina." His voice is quiet.

"I need you to check your messages."

There is silence, then a quiet buzz on his end as he opens the image I sent.

"What am I looking at?" he asks.

"One of Luciano's men," I tell him. "Or, more precisely, his brother... Or was."

There is another long beat of silence.

"Fuck, you're sure?"

"Positive. I had my guy on the street confirm it. He was still talking for Luciano, trying to keep the name alive, stirring things up with small-time crews. But..." I let the words trail off, a small smirk tugging at my lips. "Looks like he bet wrong."

Marco groans under his breath. "That's dark, Rosie."

"So is this business," I say.

He doesn't argue. He knows better.

"Listen, I need you back here. Tommy's on his way to clear the scene. We can't afford any questions."

"I'm already on route," he says. "I'll be there in ten."

"Good. And, Marco?"

"Yeah?"

"We need to talk about what happens next." I hang up before he can answer.

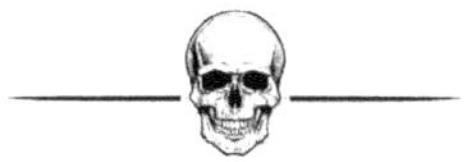

Ten minutes later, Marco pushes through the glass doors of my office. He looks like he hasn't slept, shirt rumpled, his tie loosened, and dark circles under his eyes.

Stopping in front of my desk. "You weren't fucking kidding," he says, dropping a folder onto the glass. "Tommy just called. They're already clearing the floor."

"Good, no delays. We need that casino up and running again by tonight."

He raises an eyebrow. "That soon?"

Leaning back in my chair, I cross one leg over the other. "We can't give anyone time to wonder what happened. No customers, and definitely no cops, business as usual. We're supposed to be running an empire not a circus."

He nods. "Understood. You want me to start hiring replacements?"

"Yes. Pull new staff for security, dealers, hosts, anyone we lost or let go. I don't care if they come from Atlantic City, Vegas, or the damn Bahamas. We'll train them to our standard."

Marco reaches for his phone and starts typing. "HR's got files ready to go. Dealers, floor managers, bartenders, valets...you name it. I'll have the shortlists by this afternoon."

"Make sure they're clean," I say. "No priors, no debts, no connections to the families. We can't risk another rat slipping through."

His fingers are still moving fast across the screen, but he nods again. "Got it."

I stand, pacing toward the window. "Luciano's ghost is still talking," I tell him quietly. "But now his brother's gone, that'll stop soon enough. I don't want to hear that name again."

Marco looks up. "And if someone does start whispering it?"

"Then we remind them what happens to people who do," I say simply.

He gives a small, humorless laugh. "Sounds good to me." He pockets his phone and looks up at me. "Alright, HR's moving. New recruits for dealers and floor staff should be here within four hours. We'll run background checks on everyone before they're even through the door."

"Good." I sit back down, tapping a pen against the table. "Tell security to run double shifts tonight. Cameras, tables, the vault...all of it. I don't want a whisper of this outside these walls."

He hesitates then, just for a moment. "Rosie...what about the PA?"

Meeting his eyes I tell him, "That's personal. But if you're asking whether it changes how I see you, it doesn't. You did your job when it mattered."

I can tell by the look in his eyes he doesn't believe me, but he doesn't push. After a moment of silence, my phone buzzes again. A message from Tommy.

Tommy: Scene cleared. No cops. No cameras. No leaks.

Perfect.

I look back at Marco. "Tell the dealers to be ready by nine. Tables open at ten. We go back to business."

He nods and turns toward the door.

"Marco," I call, stopping him. He looks back. "Make sure HR prioritizes the dealers and security and get the new floor manager vetted personally. I want to know everything about whoever's handling my tables."

"Understood," he says, leaving without another word.

When the door closes behind him, I finally let out the breath I hadn't realized I'd been holding. The office is quiet again. Luciano's brother is dead, the gang silenced, and the casino would open tonight like nothing ever happened. The machine would keep turning.

CHAPTER 45

Marco

RETURNING TO THE CASINO, it smelled of bleach...and death, you'll never be able to scrub it clean.

I had to hand it to them, to the customers, they'd never guess that twelve hours ago this floor looked like a crime scene. The tables gleam and the lights sparkle brightly. The dealers take their positions behind velvet ropes, all with perfect smiles on their faces. You could almost believe last night didn't happen...almost.

I stand near the pit, one eye on the dealers, the other on the new guy waiting at the blackjack tables. The new floor manager...Daryl Cooper, according to his file. Mid-forties, built like a man who still worked out before dawn. Stern face, shaved head, eyes that saw everything but gave nothing away, exactly what we needed.

His resume read like a casino's greatest hits. Floor supervision, dealer rotation, credit handling, surveillance coordination, dispute resolution, the whole fucking package. Ten years in Vegas, five in Atlantic City. Clean record, no priors, no debt, no family in the business. The kind of man you could trust with your tables and your secrets.

I walk over, extending my hand. “Daryl Cooper?”

He shakes it firmly. “Yes, sir. Pleasure.”

“Marco Romano. I run operations for this property.”

“Understood.” His tone is short, efficient. “I’ve already met your HR lead and a few of the pit bosses. I’ll make sure staff rotation runs smoothly tonight. Surveillance angles are solid, and your security chief has already shown me the feeds.”

“Good.” I nod. “I like someone who gets ahead of the job.”

“I like a place that runs tight,” he replies.

I smile faintly. “You’ll report directly to me.”

“Understood, sir.”

He doesn’t ask what happened last night. Smart man. The kind who knows better than to speak of things that aren’t in his job description. I give him a nod of approval and walk him toward the exit. “Welcome to the team, Daryl. Let’s keep this place running like the world never stopped turning.”

He smirks, just slightly. “That’s the only way to win, sir.”

When he is gone, the silence rushes back in. The sound of cards shuffling and coins clinking feels almost peaceful, like nothing had ever gone wrong.

But I can’t lie to myself, not tonight, not after what I’ve done.

I go back to my office, shutting the door behind me. On my desk sits her mug. The one she used every morning, half chipped, lipstick stain still faint on the rim.

She'd left it there to annoy me, like she did most days. I should throw it away, but I can't.

Instead, I just sit staring at it, remembering the way she'd lean on the doorway, hair loose, always smirking like she knew how much she got under my skin. It started the first day she walked into my office. Confident, sharp, and sexy as hell. I'd known right then she'd be trouble, and she was. The kind of trouble that you rewrite rules for.

I'd written that staff policy myself, no interoffice relationships, no dating, no sleeping together. I thought it'd save me, build a wall. But walls don't mean much when the person you're trying not to want works three feet from your desk and smells like vanilla and sin.

So, I did the only thing I could think of, I pushed her away. Gave her errands that didn't matter. Sent her out to collect documents, deliver packages, check on suppliers. Anything to keep her moving. Anything to keep her out of my line of sight.

And now...because of that...

I press my palms against my desk, lowering my head. She'd been at the casino because of me. Because I couldn't stand being in a room with her without wanting her, and now she was gone. The weight of it sat in my chest. I'd seen a lot of death in this life. Friends, enemies, strangers, and it all blurs eventually. But this...this one cut differently. A knock at the door breaks through my thoughts.

"Yeah?"

The door opens, and Rosie walks in first, black suit, crisp white shirt, not a single hair out of place. She looked every inch the boss she was. La Madrina. Power in heels.

Behind her, Gabe follows, silent but watchful. And then Nico—the Don himself. The air in the room drops ten degrees the second he steps in.

They didn't have to say anything. I already knew why they were here. I stand, straightening my tie, ready for it.

Rosie's gaze is steady, unreadable. Nico's jaw is tight, his usual calm replaced by a simmering frustration, and Gabe just leans against the wall, arms folded, saying nothing.

Exhaling through my nose, I look at them all. "I know," I tell them quietly. "I fucked up."

Rosie's expression doesn't change, but Nico's eyes narrow.

"I sent her there," I continue, "to the casino. I thought...fuck, I don't even know what I thought. That she'd be out of the way, that I could focus." Shaking my head, a bitter laugh escapes me. "It's fucking stupid. I wrote a damn policy to stop myself. Thought if I made it a rule, it'd fix what was in my head. But it didn't. And now she's dead because of me."

The silence is suffocating.

Rosie crosses her arms. "We all know the rules, Marco. You broke yours."

"I know," I say again, louder this time. "And I don't need to hear it. Not from anyone. Not from my old boss..." I say looking at Nico. "And not from my new one." Rosie's brows lift slightly at that. "I don't care if he's the Don and you're La Madrina," I tell them. "I can't sit here and listen to another lecture about fucking control. I know what it costs. I've paid the fucking price."

Rosie steps forward then, her tone softening just a fraction. "You lost someone who worked for you. Someone who mattered to you. That's not weakness, Marco...it's human. But don't confuse guilt with loyalty. One you carry, the other you prove."

I meet her gaze. "And how do I prove it?"

"By doing what you do best," she says. "Running my floors. Keeping my empire clean. Making sure no one ever pays that price again."

For a long moment, we just look at each other, neither saying anything, her words hanging in the silence.

Finally, I look away and tell them, "Then that's what I'll do."

And all I have left is her ghost, the scent of her perfume still clinging to the office, and the chipped coffee cup, to remind me of what I'd done.

I straighten, forcing the emotion down, locking it behind the same iron walls I'd spent years building. The show must go on.

And if guilt is the cost of control, then I'd pay it a thousand times over.

CHAPTER 46

Harper

OKAY. SO, THIS ISN'T ideal, you know those moments in life when you think, *maybe I should've called in sick*? Yeah. This is one of them.

I'm hunched over, pressing my hand against my side because, apparently, some genius thought stabbing me was a fun idea. It's not deep, but it's definitely enough to make walking feel like I'm actually running a marathon. The casino lights are still flashing behind me, the sound of the slot machines ringing in my ears as I stumble out through the side exit. Funny how they still sound cheerful. Blood trickles warm under my fingers, but from what I left behind, you'd think I was dead with the pool of blood on the ground. At least it's not gushing, so I'm counting that as a win. My favorite blouse is ruined, though. Figures. I finally wear something cute to work, and it ends up soaked in blood.

"God, Marco's gonna kill me," I mumble, half laughing, half wincing. "Not because I'm bleeding out, no. Because I didn't bring back those fucking contracts."

I can just imagine it, him standing there, in a sharp suit and that stupidly handsome scowl, saying something like *'You had one job, Harper.'*

Yeah, Marco, sorry. My bad. Got stabbed. Long story.

My laugh comes out a little wild and echo-y in the alley. That's when it hits me that I might be in shock. Or maybe I'm just too sarcastic to process trauma like a normal person. The pain spikes when I move, so I press harder on the wound and start hobbling down the sidewalk. The streetlights blur a bit. My head feels light, and my steps sound weirdly far away.

"Come on," I whisper to myself. "You've done worse hung over." That's a lie but lies are comforting.

I need to get to NIC. The one place I know, the one place where Marco will be. He's probably pacing right now, waiting for me to come back with that paperwork. He'll be pissed because, of course he will. He's always pissed. And yet...even now, bleeding and probably concussed, I can't stop thinking about him. That jawline that looks carved out of stone. The way his voice gets all low when he's trying not to yell. The fact he smells like sandalwood and danger and I kind of hate it but also...don't.

God, I'm pathetic.

I should be thinking about first aid, but no. I'm thinking about how Marco's gonna react when he sees me like this. Probably that same mix of irritation and concern he does so well. The kind that says *you're an inconvenience, but I'd kill anyone who touches you.*

And that's the problem. He never does anything about it. Just broods.

So yeah, I've been playing his little game. Doing his dumb errands. Running around Jersey like a glorified delivery girl, all to get a reaction out of him. To make him *break*. Except now...the joke's on me.

My phone's shattered...literally. The guy who stabbed me must've thought it was funny to toss it down and step on it. Cracked it clean in half, so I can't even call for help.

I keep walking or limping, whatever this motion is, it's not graceful. Every few steps I stop and lean against a wall, breathing through the pain. The city around me is totally oblivious. Traffic blares, someone's arguing two streets over. Life just keeps going, even when you're bleeding out on the sidewalk.

"Alright," I mutter, "you've survived worse dates."

The NIC building finally appears in the distance, tall, all glass and imposing. It's like a lighthouse for people with terrible life choices. By the time I reach it, the sky's gone from dusky gold to deep blue. How long have I been walking? Hours? Minutes? I've stopped counting. My feet feel like lead, and I've taken enough 'rests' against random walls to look like I'm bar hopping. The lobby lights are still on. That's good, someone is here.

I pause at the glass doors, catching my reflection. Pale face, my hair's a mess, shirt soaked, blood drying in weird patterns. Great. I look like the world's worst crime scene reenactment.

"Alright, Harper," I whisper. "Act normal. You're fine. Totally fine. You're just gonna walk in there, get a bandage, and maybe flirt with your boss before you collapse. Easy."

One deep breath, then I push through the doors. The elevator feels like it's taking forever, every second stretches, the flicker of the fluorescent lights drilling into my skull. I lean against the mirrored wall, staring at myself.

"God, he's gonna be so fucking mad," I grumble. "I can't believe I got stabbed *and* failed to get his paperwork. I'd rather face the knife again." A weak laugh escapes me. "At least the knife didn't sigh dramatically every time it looked at me."

When the elevator doors finally ding open, the hallway's empty, everyone's gone home, of course they have, it's probably late. My vision flickers. I catch myself against the wall, breathing hard.

"You're fine," I tell myself again. "You're being dramatic, you're not dying."

But my knees say otherwise, buckling under me. I catch the edge of a table outside Marco's office, the world tilting sideways. For a second, I consider just lying down right here, maybe taking a quick nap, that sounds nice. But no...he'll find me, and then I'll never live it down. I drag myself to the office door. It's slightly open, light still spilling out. He's here, of course he's here. I can hear his voice low, talking to someone. Probably Rosie or maybe Gabe. I should just walk in. Make an entrance.

'Hey, boss, guess who didn't die today?'

Yeah. That'd go over great. Except my mouth's too dry, and my legs feel like jelly. I press my hand harder against my side and take another shaky step.

"You're almost there," I whisper. "Don't pass out now. You made it this far."

My vision wavers. The lights blur. The ground tilts again.

"Marco," I try to call out, but it comes out as a whisper.

I take one more step, two, then my body just gives up. My hand slips from the wall, my knees hit the carpet, and the last thing I see is his office door swinging open. And for a split second just before everything fades, I swear I see him, that same look on his face. Shock, anger, and something else. Something softer.

Then black.

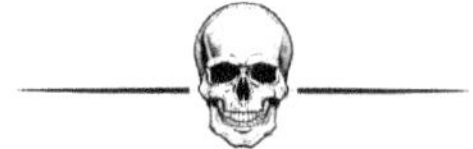

Somewhere between awake and unconscious, I hear voices.

"Get a medic."

"She's alive."

"Barely."

Figures. Still not good enough to die properly.

I want to say something snarky, but my mouth won't cooperate. All I manage is a groan.

Someone's hand presses against mine, warm, rough but familiar.

Of course it's him.

"Don't," Marco's voice says quietly. "Don't you dare."

I want to laugh. *Don't I dare what? Bleed on your carpet?*

But the world tilts again before I can finish the thought, and everything slips away.

THE END

Acknowledgements

THANK YOU SO MUCH for reading. If you have enjoyed A Mafia's Angel, please consider leaving a review, they really help out indie authors and are very much appreciated.

This book has been a challenge for me, but one I have enjoyed seeing turn from scraps of paper into what it is today. I hope you loved reading it just as much as I enjoyed creating it. A few thank you's... To my ARC Team, I can't thank you all enough for the support you have given with all your reviews, and shares, and the love you give to my books. And my readers, I have been blown away with the support I have and continue to receive, and the reviews and comments I have received have been incredible. Chris, since meeting you, you have helped me in so many ways and I can't say how much this has meant to me, you've become a true friend and confident - it's scary how we think the same things, but I love how we understand each other.

Thanks to Imogen, at From Beginning to The End, who has the unfortunate task of editing for me, but she does it with great feedback and guidance. And to Getcovers for the beautiful cover. My husband, once again, who always listens to me go on and on about this book while I have written it. I love you always. Finally, last but not least, my parents, who continually support me in all the things I want to achieve in my life.

I have to give a special mention to my Dad who helped me write the blurb, which was odd but at the same time a little funny as I'm not sure if he actually knew that's what he was doing, but was a massive help!

Thank you. I appreciate you all so much
Much love Sarah x

Also by S.E Robin

The Wicked Duet
Wicked Lies
Wicked Secrets

The Damaged Sinners of New York
A Mafia's Treasure
A Mafia's Angel
A Mafia's Sweetness – Due 2026
A Mafia's Addiction – Due 2027

Anthologies
A Sugar and Spice Anthology – Timeless Love

About The Author

Born in Cambridgeshire, I am a wife to my childhood sweetheart. A Quality Engineer and now Author. I have been aspiring to become an author for a long time. I was inspired to put my fingers to the keyboard a few years ago when I met a group of girls at Rare23 London.

We became friends and discovered that some of us had the same aspirations, we pushed each other to start up doing what we loved most and here we are today! Crazy right, but all possible. I have had several stories in my head over the years and I have enjoyed putting them all down for you to enjoy, I am really looking forward to you seeing what's next.

Some of my stories have been inspired by my adventures across Europe and the places in my books, albeit fictitious, are loosely based on places I have seen. I absolutely love picturing these places when I put them down on paper.

www.ingramcontent.com/pod-product-compliance
Lightning Source LLC
LaVergne TN
LVHW010654110826
845149LV00014B/3086